To Amara
Be blessed & stay
[gracious?] [illegible]

Embellished Truths

a novel

Embellished Truths

a novel

by

Dreas

A. J. Endeavours, LLC™
Baltimore, Maryland

For information write to:

A.J. Endeavours
Attention: Dreas
822 Guilford Avenue #122
Baltimore, Maryland 21202

(877) 95-DREAS | Fax (877) 467-9299

E-mail: dreas@dreaschimera.com
Website: www.dreaschimera.com

Cover design by C.J. (www.clove2design.com)

Thank You

I thank God for His mercy, favor, and grace, and for each and every lesson… for *I wouldn't take nothin' for my journey now! Humbled by humility!* To my editor, Ms. Taifa Peaks, I thank you for your patience, dedication, and all of the constructive criticism to which you have extended. I thank my two angels (my mother and grandmother) for the abundance of strength in which you both have left me with. I love and miss you two, more than I could have ever fathomed. To my new spiritual sisters, K.P. and A. Moses, I thank you for being my sounding board, for keeping me still, and for listening to me whine. To my life-long spiritual sisters, Kay B., Nika, and Shantia, I thank you for holding me up, when my legs were too weak to stand alone. All of you ladies, collectively, exemplify, true sista-hood at its best… and so, I thank you from the bottom of my heart. To my doe-eyed bambino… when Mommy wanted to give up, those ebony eyes pierced my soul and gave me the courage to go on. A real life *Theo & Clair*, we are... I love you, pumpkin! If I have my way, the world will be your gift! To the one who has shared much of this journey with me... *no one knows how much of our story goes untold and all the silent cries we woe'd...as our life began to unfold...* I will always love you! And to anyone who has taken this journey with me, whom I may have forgotten, please know that I also thank you. Charge my forgetfulness to my absent-mind and not my loving-heart... God Bless!

-Dreas

I once had a dog as a friend...
who said he would love me to the end...
I caught him at home—alone with some bones—
or chickens—or maybe some hens...
I screamed and I pleaded for attention...
And oh, how I hoped he would listen...
But at the end of the day-my dog went astray-
and left me with ill-filled intentions!
...hope the stain remains like a tattoo,
reminding me what not to do...
...pseudo love affairs!!!

-Dreas

Phase I:
Intuitions

1

"Hello?" I answered, half asleep.

"Wake ya ass up and tell us how dat fat pussy feel."

"*What*?!"

"Ya 'eard me. She said bet ya pussy dun get wedda den ere's," his velvety voice spoke again.

I'd finally learned how to understand his island tongue and the melodic tone I'd recognize anywhere. It was Quazi, and the tone of this man's voice alone caused me to crème in my panties. He must have been passing through my town on another business trip. Although I still wasn't quite sure how he made his living, one thing I was sure of was that if this was my greeting and he was using one hand to grip the phone, he had to be using the other to caress that long black dick of his.

"Quazi who is *she* and why you callin' me this time of night? How you know my man ain't here?

What, you tryin' to get my forehead cracked?" I questioned as I immediately began to lower the volume of my cell. I got up from bed and peeped through the window to check for Mekhi's car.

"Ma, calm down. Me know ya dere alone 'cause ya wouldna talked ta me dis long if hem were dere wit'ya. In fact, me probably wouldna even gotten tru."

"Quazi, how long you gonna be in town? I can't come out this time of night and you still haven't told me who *she* is."

"Not long... Yasmine come ova ere, she wanna talk ta ya."

"Yasmine?"

"Yes, Ma, Yasmine," he teased.

Yasmine was his Brazilian friend who I only had the privilege of seeing in pictures. But, from what I could tell, she stood around 5'9", was built like a stallion, and had an hourglass figure that would make any heterosexual woman rethink her sexual preference.

"Ma, ya know ya wan it and we're ere just waiting for ya ta come an join in. Huh, tell her what you told me eh," I overheard him say before he passed her the phone.

"*Olá, Gizelle,* you coming out to play, no?" the female voice moaned on the other end.

"*Ola, chica.* Define *play.* You sure *you* can hang?"

"I willing to try. Quazi say you got the sweetest pussy he ever taste, but I say no. You let me taste, no?"

"Mmm... Yasmine... if I *do* let you taste it, *what are you gonna do for me*?"

"...Now wait a minute," Quazi interrupted.

"Ya gotta come over da get de answer ya'self. Is ya comin' or not?"

"...huuuuh." I loudly exhaled and glanced over at the alarm clock. *2:00 a.m.* seemed to be screaming at me in big, bold red numbers. Maybe a late-night rendezvous would be just what the doctor ordered. Hell, Mekhi was obviously pulling another late-nighter anyway.

"Yeah, I'm comin'. Just give me a minute to throw something on. You at the Condo?"

"No otter place to be. Be waitin' for ya right ere."

I lay in bed pondering over the conversation I just had. Yasmine didn't have to answer my last question. I was already sold on the idea of a little ménage a trois. In fact, the anticipation of fucking her and Quazi at the same time, and before Mekhi got in, sent chills down my spine and caused me to finger my own moist lips. I had known Quazi for a while now, but only recently had he broken me out of my shell and unleashed this other side. He could take me so far out of the realm of my ordinary character and into a seductive zone that was hypnotic, sensual and captivating. It was a pleasure I had yet to experience with Mekhi.

But, Mekhi was my man. And what I was about to do with Quazi, I should've been able to do with him, but he never made me feel comfortable enough to do so. With Quazi, I could be free. Free to be myself and free to explore without any judgment. There were no roles or standards to live up to. But with Mekhi, things were different. I felt like if I didn't live up to a certain role, there would be no us, mostly because of the way he carried himself out in the streets. He was well-respected and *very* appreciated in the streets. So quite naturally I, being the female on his arm, had to follow suit in a presentable manner.

I climbed out of the huge king canopy bed while wondering what excuse I would use to explain my outing. Somewhere in the background, I heard my cell go off again.

"That fool is really pushing his luck now," I whispered under my breath.

"*Yes? Helloo…*" Shit! I hadn't even bothered to check who was calling before answering, but could now tell that the background noise was completely different from what I heard before.

"HONK…HONK!" The sound of a car horn screamed loudly through the phone.

"WHAT THE FUCK?!" the voice on the other end yelled.

"Hello, HELLO!" I said again, a little more cognizant of to whom the voice belonged. It was Mekhi.

"Oh, so YOU NOT SLEEP?! Why you ain't call me when you got in? DAMN! Never mind! I was just checkin' to see if you was in there. How long you been in the house?" Mekhi sarcastically rambled down his list of questions. *Here he goes with this shit again.* I hated when he did this shit! I felt like a teenager being drilled by one of her parents.

"Since *I* got off from work, which was exactly what *you* were suppose to do, remember?! Where are *you* and why aren't *you* here yet? You said you would be here *before* I got in."

"I BE THERE!"

I was in the middle of asking what time that would be before I noticed he was no longer on the line.

He pisses me the fuck off with that shit! Sure, *he* wanted *me* in the house at a decent hour but it was different for his ass because of "the game." The game, the game, the game! He blamed everything on the goddamn game! Giving *me* some goddamn third degree… I'd like to put his ass on the stand under oath. No telling what or who he was out there doing this time of night in them goddamn streets. Besides, what had his ass *so busy* that he hadn't called me once since

I got off from work? And it's Halloween, too! He *knew* how I felt about Halloween! It is the devil's holiday, not ours.

We lived in Baltimore Maryland, otherwise known as Bodymore-Murderland, which meant, at least in my town, Halloween only gave the fools, ghouls, and goblins an excuse to do what they were going to do anyway. Sure, Mekhi was valued in the streets, I'd give him that. Some might even go so far as to compare him with Michael Corleone. But the game was changing and the *"Godfathers"* of yester-year had been replaced by the thugs of today. Them hoodlums operated by a whole different code.

"SHIT!" I shouted out before sending Quazi a text canceling our plans. "This shit ain't right. Not him, not this relationship, and definitely not this night!" *Something just doesn't feel right about this night!* I thought to myself as I yawned and angrily crawled back into bed. I turned on my side and tried to re-focus on Martin pulling one over on Gina and Pam.

"They're so silly," I said, referring to the characters on the popular 1990's sitcom, *Martin*. As sleep began to take over my body, I grabbed my Papi bear and held it close to me before slipping into one of my recurring dreams. The visions started with the card game, just as they always did. However, tonight they seemed a little more vivid than usual. It was almost as if they were a prelude to what was about to come…

In a small row home, Julio and six of his Army buddies have gathered to play cards, have drinks, and engage in a game of Russian roulette. Mommy and I have just pulled up outside and even though the adorned window drapery clearly gives view of the outside from within, no one in the home seems to have noticed our arrival.

My mother asks, "How much do I owe you, again?"

The cab driver responds, "Six bucks. She's a cutie… takes after you. Her eyes are the shape of an Egyptian queen's. Hi, Cutie. How old is she?"

"She's…" My mother pauses to locate her purple and gold coin-filled Crown Royal bag, "…five." She picks up the bag and begins to count aloud six dollars in change. I sit and quietly watch, secretly knowing that those coins were part of the reason why we were there. Mommy must have been low on dollars and needed to re-up on cash. "A lady always keeps a hidden stash," she would preach to me over and over again.

"Here you are. Thank you," she says while leaning forward to pay the driver. "Say thank you, Gizelle, and come on."

"Thank you… okay… Mommy I'm comin'," I respond as I glance up at my mother's beautiful golden complexion and bright hazel eyes. Her good looks were

only half the reason she received so much attention. Her curvaceous figure was responsible for the other half. She was perfection at its best and she had every man thanking her creator for such a well put together package.

As we exit the cab, a cool late summer breeze blows pass, as I grip one of my mother's hands with my right hand and tightly hold on to my teddy bear with the other.

"Okay, baby, when we get in there I want you to give your Papi Julio a big hug and kiss okay?"

"Okay, Mommy," I reply, but neither one of us was prepared for what would happen next.

"Oh, okay so y'all think I won't do it huh? And gon' bet against me? Y'all should know by now not to bet against this crazy ass Puerto Rican," my father practically yells as he puts the 40 ounce to his mouth with his left hand, and grasps the thirty-eight revolver with his right. He places the gun to his temple as the other card players begin to chant, "1, 2... 1, 2..."

As Mommy and I approach the door, I excitedly look up at her as she goes to knock, but she doesn't get a chance to. Instead the door spills open just as the group reaches, "3!"

As my mother and I enter into the home, a single gunshot rings out. There we stand, watching as the beer bottle falls, breaks, and glass splatters across the floor. Cards fly in the air and so does everything inside my Papi's head.

There I stand watching as his bronze, muscular, 6'3" frame tumbles to the floor; his dark brown eyes piercing through me the entire time. I can't move. I hold on to my bear as tight as I can and watch while my mother and his friends rush to his aid.

Left in the doorway, I stand with my hands covering my ears, but it didn't matter what I could hear. The fact was I had just witnessed the whole horrific scene. Less than ten feet away was my Daddy, dead from a self-inflicted gunshot wound in his head.

There was so much blood and so much commotion. It was as if time had stopped and everything and everybody inside the room was in slow motion trying to correct an uncorrectable condition. The paramedics come and work on him, but it's hopeless. He's already dead. In an instant my Dad has been taken away from me and looking into my mother's eyes, essentially I've lost a part of her, too.

I watch her on her knees, screaming and crying hysterically, rocking back and forth rapidly and shaking and breathing uncontrollably. At this moment, it seems as if nothing and no one can calm her. Half of the card players try and the other half, well they need comforting themselves. Between them and my mother, I'm not sure who cried the most.

It's also unclear who or when it was determined that I was in the doorway and didn't need to witness more of the horrendous tragedy in the making. Some-one finally came, picked me up and carried me out-side. Away from the home, away from the dreadful scene, and away from my Papi forever...

Outside of the home, I sat on someone's lap. In my dream I can never make out a face, but it really didn't matter as my thoughts were no longer there, but rather, forming recurring visions of loneliness and a love lost that would forever disturb me. I look back at the house once more, the door still wide open and I can hear my mother scream, "God, NO! Gizelle, NOOOO..."

--BOOM!!!...And just like that, I'm back in my bedroom with Martin, Gina, and Pam.

2

The slam of a car door woke me from my dream and brought me right back to the shenanigans on *Martin*.

I bet that's him. Hmm, what will it be tonight? I'm sure he's contrived something to get himself out of this one. I know him like a book. He'll come in, tap me on my shoulder and try to state his case. Then he'll complain how I never understand that when he's out in the streets, he's conducting business and ain't hardly thinkin' about no bitches. Then, when he sees that I ain't going for it, he'll start to whine for a dose of me hoping that I'll eventually give in, pounce on top of him and fuck his brains out. But, tonight his ass is sadly mistaken if he thinks he's getting anything other than a cold stare and a heated argument. He has some nerve. Hadn't this been the very subject of our argument this morning? I'm so sick of his bullshit. Does he really think he's the only one who can play this game? Oohh! Just wait, I'll show his ass!

The familiar hum of his engine pulling into the parking lot caused me to back track a little.

Oh, that's him? *Well who in the hell just slammed a car door this time of night?* I thought to myself. Halloween or not, this was usually a pretty quiet neighborhood, especially with it being so late. I got up and peeped out the window. When the shine of his familiar BMW's halogen lights confirmed my suspicion that it was indeed Mekhi, I started mentally preparing myself for all that I had waiting for him.

"BOOM, BOOM, BOOM!" came from the hallway.

It sounded as if someone had either fallen down the stairs or dropped a bag of canned goods down the four flights leading up to our apartment. Not only is he late, but now he has to let the whole building know it, by making a goddamn spectacle of himself. Now wait a minute, it was damn near 3 a.m. and I could think of a lot of words to describe my man, and clumsy would not be one of them. I immediately jumped up and headed straight towards the front door, praying all the while that everything was okay. Yet, somewhere deep inside I already knew that it wasn't. As I approached the door I could hear a few strange voices coming from the other side, but there was only one

I could make out clearly and that voice belonged to Mekhi.

I put my ear to the door to confirm what my mind had already calculated to be A FUCKING ROBBERY IN PROGRESS! Shit! I looked through the peephole, but could only see the blur of a masked man before my view was covered. My breathing intensified and I began to panic as the rumbling on the other side grew louder.

Shit, think Gizelle. Think and be cool, your man needs you right now. My inner voice said.

Be cool? BE COOL? How in the hell was I supposed to be cool when my Clyde was in desperate need of his Bonnie to save the day? I thought about yanking the goddamn door open, but then suddenly remembered the words Mekhi had preached to me over the years, "If it ever came down to a robbery, leave me be! This is my world, my doings, not yours."

However, right now, none of that shit seemed to matter. In fact, any pre-rehearsed strategies went out the window as I attempted to cope with the reality of my man being in harm's way. If anything happened to him, I didn't know what I would do.

"Lord, please help us," I said as I exhaled and slowly unlocked the deadbolt. I placed my ear to the door and reached for the doorknob just as I overheard Mekhi say, "No, I told you I don't live here... I... I..."

"God be with us," I whispered to myself as I twisted the knob, but the door didn't open. I pulled it again, and still nothing. Beads of sweat began to run down my face as I frantically tugged and pulled, but still it wouldn't budge.

I looked through the peephole, but only saw darkness.

Fuck! It's not rocket science, Gizelle, just open the goddamn door! I said to myself as I tugged and tugged, but still the door wouldn't budge. It seemed as if someone was holding it from the other side because no matter what I did, or how much I pulled, it wouldn't open. In fact, nothing I tried seemed to be working right then.

Breathe, Gizelle. You can do this. You've only opened this door a million FUCKING TIMES BEFORE, SO WHAT'S SO FUCKING HARD ABOUT DOING IT NOW...

"*POP! POP!*" Two shots rang out and the commotion, the whispers, the voices, the pleads, all came to a halt. I quivered and turned the knob once more and just like that, the door opened. Without thinking, I stepped out into the hallway, not caring who or what was waiting for me on the other side.

3

The arguments, the fussing, the lies, and the rendezvous, all seemed minute as I walked into the open space in front of me. And, as my eyes locked with those of the 6-foot-tall frame that had just exited the building, my heart dropped at the sight of the body lying to the left of me.

"Ahh! Ohhh, they shot me!" Mekhi hollered out.

"OH MY GOD, SHIT! I COULDN'T GET THE DOOR OPEN! OH GOD, I'M SORRY…" I said while grabbing my head and pacing the floor. I was starting to panic all over again. "I'm so sorry, baby. Oh God, I swear I'm so sorry…" I said again before I disappeared back inside to grab the cordless phone and dial for help.

"…911 operator, do you need the police, ambulance, or the fire depart…"

"HELLO… HELLO! Please come quick, my boyfriend has just been shot!"

"Ma'am is the gunman still with you?"

"No, but he's out in the parking lot."

"Okay, where are you located?"

I gave the operator my name and address just before it hit me that this bastard was about to get away.

"Oh God, please send somebody… he's gonna get away!" I screamed out loud.

"Ms. Sadiq, can you still see him?"

"YES!"

"What kind of ca-----?"

"…He's in a four-door car with tinted windows…"

"Okay, but can you see the color and make of the car?"

"Its blue, no, no, it's black. It's either blue or black."

"Got it! Do you know what kind of car it is?"

"I… I… I don't know, a Camry. No, no maybe it's a Honda. I don't know. It's a new car, but not new, new, but not real old. I don't know… can you just hurry up and send somebody please!"

"I've already dispatched someone and they should be there shortly. Where is the victim now?"

"He's right here on the floor."

"Okay don't move him. The paramedics and police are on their way."

"I'm not, but please tell them to hurry up and come."

"Ma'am, is he still conscious?"

"Yes, BUT THEY STILL HAVE TO HURRY!"

"They're en route and should be there any minute now. Where on his body was the victim shot?"

I was becoming frustrated with the operator's questions. If they would just hurry up and get there, they would know what type of car it was, where he was lying, and where he had been shot. Nevertheless, I turned to Mekhi and asked, "Where were you shot?"

"...it feels like it's in my kidneys and...in...my leg."

"OH God...OH GOD! He says his kidneys and leg. I couldn't get the door open! Oh my God!" I exclaimed as I started pacing again.

"Can you give me a description of what the gunman looked like?"

"Um...he was tall and in all blac..."

"Tell her it was two of them. One was around 5'8" and the other, about 6 feet."

"Got it! Can you tell me a little bit more about what happened?" the operator asked after I relayed the details Mekhi had just given me.

"I don't know. It was a robbery. WHAT'S TAKING THEM SO LONG TO GET HERE?" I curtly responded.

What more did she want me to say? My boyfriend needed a fucking paramedic, a doctor, and possibly a Medivac to air lift him to shock trauma. What part of that shit needed explaining? The goddamn local news reporter seemed to always deliver a breaking story concerning the use of a Medivac, so why wasn't the same sense of urgency being executed right now?

"They should be there in a matter of minutes. You're doing great so far, Ms. Sadiq. Please try and remain calm."

"REMAIN CALM?"

"Baby… I'm getting cold," Mekhi said, his eyes rolling into the back of his head.

"NO… NO! Mekhi… you gotta stay with me. Mekhi? Mekhi!"

"I… I want you to know that I love the hell out of you."

"MEKHI… MEKHI! NNNOOOOO! OH GOD, PLEASE SEND SOMEBODY NOW!"

"The paramedics are on their way. Do you see them yet?"

"No and he's getting cold and going in and out of it. THEY GOTTA COME NOW!"

"Tell him to stay with you, Ms. Sadiq, and let him know that help is on the way."

"Baby, always remember… I… I… love…" Mekhi started again.

"I love you, too, but MEKHI… MEKHI? I need you to stay with me… baby, please," I said as I knelt down beside him.

"Ms. Sadiq, is he still conscious?"

"Yes, but why aren't they here yet? They should be here by now!"

I screamed out loud enough to wake all of my so-called sleeping neighbors. Just then, sirens began to sound around me.

"I CAN...I CAN HEAR SOME-THING... THEY'RE COMING!" I shouted out.

"Okay, can you see them yet?"

"No... no I don't see anybody... wait... wait... I can see them! I can see them now! Here they are."

"Can they see you? Make sure they can see you, Ms. Sadiq!" the operator said emphatically.

"YES, OKAY. I'm here! We're right here!" I said, as I waved my hands in the air and ran down the first flight of stairs.

"Can they see you now?"

"YES, THEY'RE COMIN' IN!"

"Okay, you can hang up now."

I ended my call with the dispatcher and instantly began to search the phone's memory for Jeremy's number. Jeremy was Mekhi's best friend.

"Who you callin'?" Mekhi asked.

"Jeremy," I answered as the call connected.

"Hello... Hello?" Jeremy's girlfriend answered.

"Tracey, TRACEY! Mekhi just got shot!"

"WHAT! Oh my God... where are you?"

"We're at the apartment."

"Okay, we're coming now!"

"You gotta come quick! Are you on your way?"

"Yes, we're coming right now."

The line went dead as my eyes met up with the first officer who had just entered the building. I didn't know what it was, but there was something about his stare that sent chills down my spine and made me realize that I didn't have any pants on. I rushed back inside and threw on the first pair of sweats that I saw.

"Hello... ma'am?" one of the officers called out from the bottom of the stairs.

"Yes, we're up here. Can you come up here, please?" I pleaded.

As the officers made their way up to the third floor and I started to give my account of the night's events, I got another strange feeling. There was something about the way those motherfuckers were looking past me and sizing me and mine up that just didn't feel right.

4

It was all a dream…

It was a hot summer day and we had all gathered to play a game of kickball in our neighborhood alley. For as long as I could remember, this had been our preferred place to play and today was no different than any other. There was the normal gang: Brianna, Michael, Kiera, Trina, Tiese, and myself, of course. We were all having a good time until Trina deemed it necessary to start her usual daily nonsense.

"Y'all just being a bunch of sore losers," I said to the opposing team members, particularly Trina.

"Nun-uh, that's y'all," Trina sharply shot back.

"*We* ain't no losers. *WE* won."

"Y'all ain't won nothin' and you just mad anyways."

"Anyways nun-uh… Y'all wanna play again?" I asked everybody else, all the while dismissing Trina's comments. I was trying my best to ignore her, but she was the only one who continued to speak up.

"We ain't playin' nothin' and we 'specially ain't playin' wit' you no mo' cause ya mutha' do drugs," Trina maliciously said while adding a twist of her neck and a roll of her eyes.

"Ooohhhh…" the other kids said in unison.

"No she don't either and you betta' take it back before I…"

"Before you what? I ain't takin' nothin' back and you betta' get your finger outta my face 'cause my mutha' ain't dead yet and she sho' ain't no drug usah like…"

"*SMACK!*" I landed a big fat hand slap right across Trina's face.

"FIGHT… FIGHT… FIGHT!" the crowd began to chant.

We were both fumbling around using every fighting technique ever taught to us and I was getting the best of her, until I fell backwards and she landed on top of me. Instantly, she had the upper hand.

"Oww… get off of me you fat whale!" I screamed out.

"No. Let go of my hair."

"You let go of mine. Owww…"

"The both of you let go right now!" Tiese's grandmother squealed as she pulled us apart. The little old lady must have heard the commotion and came out to see exactly what was going on. I felt bad that she caught us fighting, but I didn't feel bad about the fight. Trina's instigating butt had gotten just what she deserved and judging from her busted knee, I had gotten her good too.

"You two betta' put a stop to this foolishness right now and I mean *right now*! Now I knew somethin' or 'nother was going on out here, but I would've never guessed you'd be out here tryin'a tear each other apart," Tiese's grandmother continued.

"She started it…talkin' bout we losers!" Trina shouted out.

"I ain't start nothin', that was you," I said.

"Look, I don't care who started what. If you can't play nice then you don't need to be playin' at all. Why don't you all go home and take a nap anyways, try it again a little later. *Hmm.* And Tiese, you come on in here. I may not be 'sponsible for all the others and they foolishness, but you I am 'sponsible for."

"Ohhh, Grandma, how come I gotta go in? I wasn't the one fightin'."

"I was just about to come and get you anyway, so you come right on along, chile."

"But Grandma, how come I can't play for just a little while longer?"

"Well it seems to me playtime has ended. Now come along, you can come back out a little later after you've rested."

"But Grandma, Trina started it and so Gizelle pushed…"

"TIESE! Now don't you go tryn'a get cute with me, young lady. I don't wanna hear anotha' thang 'bout who started what and who pushed who. You come on in this house right now and that's that!" the little old lady said while pointing towards her home, her stare fixed on Tiese. Tiese angrily stomped towards the house, but not before rolling her eyes at our entire crowd. I didn't care, I rolled my eyes right back at her. Right now, I was mad at all of them. Not one of them tried to break up the fight, so the way I saw it, it was just as much their fault as it was mine.

As Tiese and her grandmother made their way into their home, Trina's mother called out from down the alley, "Trina… Trina… come run to the store for me."

"…aawww, man, how come I always gotta go to the store… comin'," she answered back.

"UGLY!" Trina turned my way and said, and then took off before I had a chance to respond.

By now, I was ready to go, too. The truth was my feelings had been hurt by the comments that were made and so I turned to my now former friends and said, "Give me back my ball."

"What's wrong, Gizelle?" Kiera walked over to me and asked.

"Awww man, y'all already know what's wrong with her. Trina gone say all dat stuff 'bout somebody's mutha'. She always startin' somethin'. Why you listen to her anyway? You know how she is," Michael commented.

"Yeah, dat's why I ain't even playin' wit' her no more," Brianna added.

"Y'all right. She *is* always startin' somethin' and I ain't playin' wit' her either'," Kiera piped in.

"Y'all so 'two-faceded'," I said.

"See, why you gotta go and take it out on us? We ain't done nothin' wrong."

"I ain't takin' it out on nobody. I'm ready to go home."

"Well gone an' be dat way den."

"I will!" I said, as I took off.

Who needs them anyway? They all make me sick. I said to myself as I made my way home, all the while replaying the argument over and over again in my head. I had gotten myself so worked up that I couldn't help but cry. I guess my emotion had spilled over because by the time I got to my front door, I opened the screen and then slammed it shut without thinking. I knew my grandmother wasn't home yet, so she wouldn't be able to save me from my mother's wrath.

"WHO SLAMMED THAT GODDAMN DOOR?" my mother screamed up from the basement.

"MMMAAAAAA, MAAAA!!!!" I yelled.

"GIRL, what's wrong wit' you?" my mother said, as she came rushing towards me.

"TRINA SED YOUDODRUGSSO I HITHERDEN…TIESE GRANDMUTHA GONECOME OUT…DENTHEYALLGONESIT ROUNDANDSTART TALKINBOUTMEANDGONE ALLTRYAND STILLBEMYFRIEND AND SO I LEFTCUZ THEYALLSOTWOFACEDED …"

"WAIT A MINUTE, WAIT A MINUTE! Now just calm down. What I tell you 'bout ramblin' off… can't nobody understand you when you just rattle off at the mouth like that, barely taking breaths. Now, who was fightin' and what's all this talk about somebody doin' drugs?"

"We was all playin' in da alley, so den Trina an dem started losin' and she gon' say you do drugs in front of everybody, so I hit—" My story was interrupted by the howl of my baby godbrother's cry.

"SHIT! That boy always cat nappin'. I just laid his butt down. I thought I'd be finished my last load by the time he got up. Zella, I done told you 'bout slammin' that goddamn door, that's probably what woke his butt up. I'm comin', I'm comin',￼" my mother said as she made her way up the stairs. I sat there on the top of the stairs to rest my nerves.

"Oh, I should've punched you harder, you ugly fat pig." I said while making a fist and punching my other hand. Just then, I suddenly noticed a few pieces of candy beside a pile of sorted clothes at the bottom of the stairs. I began to finger the candy to see which one I would eat first, when my attention quickly shifted to several two inch straws that were nearby on the floor. One by one, I picked them up wondering where the powdered candy was that the straws were usually used for.

"*BINGO!*" I said, as I bent down and grabbed the tiny Ziploc bag which was filled with a white sugary substance. I loved candy and this kind would be a first for me. But, as I went to open the bag, I heard my mother shout, "GIZELLE... GIZELLE! COME HERE AND HELP ME WITH THIS BOY!"

"Yeeessss, I'm comin'," I answered while quickly dashing up the stairs, leaving my new findings behind.

"*AAWW, SHIITT*! Here... come sit with this boy for a minute," my mother said as she frantically opened the dresser drawers and shook the pockets of her summer dress.

"What's wrong, Ma?"

"Nothin', just sit here with him until I get back," she said before taking off so fast that she tripped down a few stairs in her haste. I wondered what could've gotten her so upset and made a mental note never to slam the screen door again. It seemed like an hour had passed before she returned, but when she did, she was noticeably much happier.

"Ma, did you find it?" I asked, but from a distance I could hear another voice asking the same question.

"...*Did you find it? Did you see anything over there?*" the voice asked again. It was coming from another room. I slowly opened my eyes and noticed several officers roaming around my goddamn apartment wearing gloves. I lifted my head from the dining room table. Boy, did I have a headache. I went to grab my temples, but couldn't when suddenly I remembered why--I was hand-cuffed.

"*FUCK!*" I said, as it all began to come back to me.

5

"Uncuff her. There's no need for all of that," the head detective said as he walked into my apartment. The female officer nearest me immediately followed his command. My eyes darted around the room and it all started to come back to me. It had now been hours since the first two officers, Patton and Brenton, arrived on the scene. I remembered the strange feeling I had as they introduced themselves...

"This is Officer Patton and I'm now here with the victims and the Medical Response Unit," the first officer reported over his walkie talkie.

"How many times were you shot?" one of the medical attendants asked, as she immediately went to work on Mekhi.

"Twice. Once in my leg and once in my side. It kinda feels like it's in my kidneys," Mekhi answered.

"Hi, I'm Officer Brenton. What happened here?" the other officer turned to me and asked.

"My boyfri…" I began, but Mekhi quickly interrupted.

"I was hangin' out and two guys must have followed me here. Actually, now that I think about it, on my way over here, they almost hit my car driving the wrong way down a one way. I had to swerve and honk to keep them from hitting me."

"So they followed you *here*? And *you live here*?"

"No, I do," I answered.

"But, you do know this gentleman right?"

"Yes, he's my boyfriend." I didn't divulge any particulars about our living arrangement because it had nothing to do with the issue at hand. I listened intently as my man gave his account of what had gotten us to this point.

"I put everything I had with me in a bag I had in my trunk."

"What was in the bag?"

"A sweat suit, a few jackets, and a few dollars I won from gambling with some friends."

"Now, I need you to be as still as possible, okay? This may pinch a little," one of the attendants said, as he proceeded to give Mekhi a needle.

"Actually, I think it would be better if we removed your pants. Do you mind if we cut them off?"

"No… do whateva' you have to," Mekhi answered.

"Is he gonna be all right?" I asked.

"We're certainly going to do everything possible to see to it." Another attendant spoke up as they began to cut Mekhi's pants from off of him. As his pants were lifted, about five hundred dollars, in small bills, fell from his pockets and onto the floor.

"Gizelle, get my stuff, please."

"Okay."

"Woo... whoa, hold it! You can't touch that. That money is now part of our crime scene evidence," one of the officers said rather harshly, before shaking the money from my hands.

"Okay, no problem," I answered while dropping the loose money I had just gathered, back on the floor. If he was looking for a challenge, he wouldn't get it from me. What did I care about a few measly dollars?

"We're also going to need a report from you explaining exactly what took place. You can put the information on here," the other officer said, as he handed me a clipboard and a sheet of paper.

"Patton... we're going to start transporting him now. He's losing a lot of blood," one of the attendants called out.

"Okay, we'll take it from here," Patton responded.

I immediately dropped the clipboard, tossed on the first pair of sneakers I saw and grabbed my keys. But, as I started to leave, Officer Brenton stopped me and said, "Ma'am we have a few more questions before you can go."

"Here… here's what I wrote. Where are they taking him? Baby, I'm comin'!" I hollered down the stairs, as I attempted to hand the officer his template back.

"Shock Trauma," one of the medical attendants answered.

My heart pounded rapidly against my chest as I watched my man being carried into the back of the ambulance and only then did I notice Tracy and Jeremy standing in the parking lot. I motioned for them to come up, but judging from Tracy's solemn response and the police officers huddled around her, she had already tried.

I looked down at the spot where Mekhi had been lying and saw little pieces of what had to be his insides, all over the floor. Up until now I hadn't realized just how much blood he had lost.

"What else do you need from me?" I frantically questioned.

"We just have a few more questions. Who did you say lived here again?"

"Me."

"Do you have an ID we can see?"

"Yeah." Reluctantly I went to dig it out of the Prada bag I had carried earlier that day. I didn't like the way this was headed. Instead of the two officers leaving from out of my apartment, more officers started to come in. The problem was, the crime had happened on the outside of my home, not the inside. They were all getting a little bit too comfortable for me; looking over any and everything in plain eye's view. I began to scan the apartment my damn self, just to make sure I didn't see anything crazy lying around. No telling what these motherfuckers were up to.

"Wow, this is a lot of stuff. You sure have a lot of things," one of the officer's commented.

"Your boyfriend was on his way over here kind of late, don't you think?" asked another.

"No, I don't. That's what boyfriends do," I answered.

"Is this all his stuff?" another officer asked, as he fingered through some of the leather coats hanging on the outside of the living room closet.

"No. Can I leave now?"

"*No!*" came from one of the officers.

"What about the mess on the floor?" questioned another.

"What *mess*?" I snapped back, as I started to pick up some of the papers they were referring to.

"Ms. Sadiq, we need you to leave that stuff there."

"Okay. Just let me grab my keys so I can get down to the hospital!" I huffed and threw the papers back down.

"Look, we need you to calm down because you may not be leaving here at all. We could just lock you up!"

"WHAT?! Lock me up for what? And don't tell me to calm down in my own house. My boyfriend is on his way to Shock Trauma, you're denying me to go, and now you wanna play twenty-one goddamn questions. Are you *crazy*?" I said, as my voice started to escalate. Why in the world was this jackass giving me such a hard time? I knew from the beginning I didn't like him. What in the world was he hinting around? An hour later, I found my answer as I sat handcuffed to one of my dining room chairs. Supposedly, I had caused too much of a ruckus, running off at the mouth. I couldn't believe this shit.

A calmer officer came in, introduced himself as Detective Cattle Wright, and asked the officer I had been arguing with to step outside and cool down.

"Good," I thought to myself. Maybe now we could finally wrap this shit up and I could go.

"Why don't you come over here and have a seat, Ms. Sadiq?"

"What I wanna do is go and be with my boyfriend. Why can't I leave?"

"We just have a few more questions to ask you before you can go."

"But, I've already answered all of your questions. I even wrote a report. Why can't you get the information from there?"

"It's a little bit more complicated than that, Ms. Sadiq. I have to ask and I want you to be completely honest with me. Did you shoot your boyfriend?"

"What! You can't be serious?"

"I'm afraid, I'm very *serious*."

"My boyfriend just told all of *them* what happened and so did *I*."

"I hear what you're saying, Ms. Sadiq, but something just doesn't add up here. I need you to let me know if there is anything you may be hiding in here."

"What! I'm not hiding anything in here."

"...So there's nothing else you want us to see?"

"What the hell are you talkin' about? You already see everything in here."

"What it all boils down to, Ms. Sadiq, is that we think you shot your boyfriend. Now if you would just give me the gun, you'll make it a lot easier on yourself."

"WHAT GUN?! I didn't shoot my boyfriend! Look, I need to go and be with my man, so you and your crew gotta go." I said loud enough for everyone to hear. And here I thought he would be the sane one.

I should have known better! I had heard enough and now knew exactly where this was going. I only prayed the extent of my thoughts wouldn't become reality.

"Ms. Sadiq, we need to search this apartment," the detective forcefully said a minute later.

FUCK! I knew it was coming, but what rights did they have since no crime had been committed inside of my home?

"Search it for what? My boyfriend is laying up bleeding to fucking death and this is what you say to me? Nothing happened in here. Can't you tell that from the blood outside in the hallway? I couldn't even get the goddamn door open for Christ's sake! I gotta go and since you don't have my permission to be in here, you gotta go, too. In fact, all of y'all gotta go!"

"You can leave, but we're staying right here and we're going to search this apartment. We'll leave after the other detectives get here."

"*Other detectives?* And how long is that gonna be?"

"They've already been dispatched and should be here shortly. Why don't you want us to search your apartment if you're not hiding anything?"

"Why? Why do you need to, if nothing happened in here? I've seen shows about dirty cops. How do I know you won't plant somethin' in here? You weren't in here five minutes before you started accusing me of shooting my man after *we* told you exactly what happened! And you want me to trust you enough to leave you alone in here? That's crazy! Look, I gotta go."

"And you can go."

"Good," I said moving towards the front door.

"… but, we're staying right here. This has now become a crime scene," the detective coolly stated.

"Then you can wait outside."

"No, Ms. Sadiq, we need to wait right here."

"Well, then I'm not leaving. Why can't you wait in the hallway?"

"Ms. Sadiq, we have to wait in here for the others."

"And how long is that supposed to take? You said *that* 15 minutes ago!" Just then my phone rang.

"Hello?"

"Gizelle, what in the world is going on in there and why haven't you come out yet?" Tracy asked, sounding a little annoyed.

"Because they're up here accusing me of shootin' Mekhi!"

"What! Didn't you tell them what happened?"

"Yeah, and so did he, but now they're saying I shot him and that they need to search my apartment."

"What! So they're up there making shit up?"

"Yes! *Exactly!*"

"They're down here questioning us, too."

"See, this is ridiculous, why in the world would they be questioning y'all?"

"Because they're crazy!"

"It's about twelve of them in here right now peeking through my things."

"Do they have a warrant?"

"No, and they don't have my permission to be in here, either! I asked them to leave, but they won't. They're up here getting comfortable. I need a lawyer. I need to know my rights."

"It's mighty funny that you aren't hiding anything, but *now* you need a lawyer," the detective interjected.

"And they're all in my goddamn PHONE CONVERSATION, TOO! Like *I* was saying, *I need* a lawyer; I feel like my rights are being violated."

"Okay, I'm on it. I'll call you back."

I sat on one of my living room chairs. I needed these crooked assholes out of my apartment and out of my business *immediately*. I saw no need for them to be in here, especially when they showed no signs of being on my side.

"Hey, Pennington, I have to run down to the car for a second, but I want you to stay here with Ms. Sadiq. Don't let her out of your sight, even if she has to go to the bathroom. Better yet, where's Strawbridge? Anyone know if Officer Strawbridge is still around?" the detective called out.

"Yeah, be there in a sec," a rough female voice responded from the hallway.

"What's up?" A short, unattractive stocky woman, sporting a sharp bob cut appeared from out of the blue. Her look and demeanor said she wasn't to be played with.

"I need you to stay here and watch Ms. Sadiq while I run downstairs. Wherever she goes, you go, even the bathroom."

"Sure thing, whatever I can do to help," she answered.

I didn't say a word. In fact, I made up my mind from that point on to keep my mouth shut and my words guarded. These assholes weren't playing fair at all and still, for the life of me, I couldn't understand how things had spiraled downward to this point so quickly. Two weeks ago I was house hunting. Now, all in a matter of minutes, my man had been shot, I had been blamed, and I had the Law in my house waiting for word to comb through my shit. Shit like this wasn't supposed to happen; not to us and especially not to me. Hadn't we followed all the rules? I waited for someone to wake me, but this wasn't one of my wild dreams. This was my reality.

I was too stunned to cry, too smart to speak, and too paralyzed to move. All I could do was wait. Everything passes in time, that I'd come to realize while mourning my mother's death a few years back. But, what I also realized was that I had to live in the moment to get through it and that was the part that could be painful as hell. Nevertheless, I guess this was *my* moment.

Thirty minutes later, a sarcastic-looking, blonde-haired man of average height walked in carrying a leather binder and sporting several badges around his neck.

"Hi, I'm Detective Shifton and you must be Ms. Sadiq?" he said to me.

"Yes, I am."

"I have a few questions for you, if you don't mind."

I answered all of his preliminaries: where I lived, how long I'd been a resident at my current address, how I knew the victim, what his relationship was to me, etc, etc, etc. But, it was his last question that threw me for a loop. The detective stared at me and unapologetically asked, "Do you know that your boyfriend is a drug dealer?"

"What?! No, he isn't. First they say I shot him, now he's a drug dealer. Which one is it?"

"Where do you think all of that money came from?"

"All of what money?"

"All of the money lying in the hallway."

"He was out gambling, he already told them that."

"Yeah, but don't you think that was a bit much, Ms. Sadiq?"

"No, but I think you and your crew are! And, I think this whole night is a bit much! I believe my man. Hell, I saw the robbers myself."

"That's still a lot of money that fell and..."

"A lot of money for whom? Why are we being targeted when..."

"...my background and experience lead me to the conclusion that it is drug money. We're going to need to search your home, Ms. Sadiq."

"Search it for what? He doesn't even live here!" I was getting nowhere fast with these jerks so I had to switch up my argument. This idiot had been in my home all of five minutes and already we fit the goddamn profile of the drug dealer and hustler's girl.

"What's his address?"

"I can't remember off-hand I believe it's 3771, but he lives on Pickanoo Road."

"Why don't you want us to search your home?"

"Because nothing happened in here. What I want is for y'all to leave. I don't give you or anybody else my permission for any type of search. In fact, you don't have my permission to be in here at all. I need you to leave. Will you please leave?"

"We're not going anywhere and we're going to search this apartment with or without your consent."

"Well, you're gonna need a warrant because you definitely don't have my consent!"

"Okay, then I'll go get one and bring it back," the detective said before disappearing again.

There I sat waiting for a miracle to come and feeling alienated for the first time in my own space. For so long, this space had been my own private sanctuary-providing comfort and serenity. But right now I felt like the odd man out. I sat and watched the remaining officers peek into my personal belongings; not searching, but desperately wanting too, and suddenly I felt deeply violated. What they were waiting for was merely a couple of words of confirmation for them. But for me, it could possibly destroy all that I had come to know as being normal.

I sat there for the next few hours trying desperately to make sense of it all. Before long, Detective Shifton returned carrying two white notices.

"Okay fellas, I'm back. Ms. Sadiq here are the warrants you requested," he sang out, shoving the papers in my face.

Ain't that a bitch! Now it's what I requested? If I remembered correctly, I had no choice in the matter.

"Do you have any questions for us?"

"No," I dryly answered.

"Okay then, you can go, unless you fellas have more questions for her."

"No," they all answered one by one.

"Okay. Well, here's my card. If you have any questions or any other information to lend, please don't hesitate to call."

As I turned to leave I could already hear the orders being called out about how the raid was to be executed. *Damn, Mama never said there would be days like this!*

Out in the hallway, the yellow tape and bullet shell casings confirmed the night I had just had. It felt like it took me forever to get down the goddamn stairs. I tried not to run, but I was so scared the detectives would change their minds and ask me to come back, that I couldn't help but skip a few. I had been sitting in the gloomy, depressing-ass atmosphere of my apartment for so long that I hadn't realized just how bright and clear it had become outside. The sun was so bright that I had to shield my eyes in order to find Tracy's car.

"Gizelle, I'm over here," Tracy called out while motioning for me to come and join her.

"So, they finally let you come out, huh? Jeremy left a while ago. Well... what's going on in there now?" Tracy asked as I slipped into the back seat of her car.

"They just started the raid. Those bitches! They told me I could leave, so I left. Were you able to get a lawyer?" I asked.

"Yeah, but he basically said they would do what they wanted to do now and everything else would need to be ironed out in court later. He asked me if everything was all right in there, I told him yeah, but now I'm asking you: *Is everything all right in there?*"

"Who you askin'? I don't know," I said still feeling a bit shocked by all that was going on. "Is that the only advice he could give?"

"Yeah, basically that's it in a nut shell."

"Shit! Has anybody heard from Mekhi yet?"

"No, not yet, but I know word has started to spread because my cell has been buzzin'."

"Figures."

"You ready to go?"

"Yeah… wait …FUCK!"

"WHAT?! What's wrong?"

"I gotta go back in. I forgot somethin'," I said as my eyes darted across the parking lot.

"You sure, Gizelle?"

"Yeah, I'm positive, but just in case I don't come back out, here are all of my keys," I said as I slipped one key off of the ring and gave Tracy all the others.

"Okay, but *you are* coming back out, right?"

"I hope so, girl," I said as I dashed from her car, nervous as hell about being seen. I was heading straight for the storage unit at the bottom of the hallway stairs. I had just unlocked the locks when I heard voices coming from the upstairs hallway.

Shit! Two officers were making their way down the stairs, heading right in my direction. Fuck, did they see me come back in? They would certainly lock my ass up if they saw what I was in the process of doing.

Desperately, I tried to squeeze inside of the small storage space, but it was of no use. The space wasn't big enough to hold me.

"*Hey!*" a voice called out.

…My heart stopped beating and beads of sweat ran down my forehead as I waited to hear what would come next.

"I need you two back up here for a minute. You gotta' come check this out," the voice continued. The two officers immediately U-turned and headed back up the stairs.

I silently thanked God before frantically searching the dark space again. *"Bingo!"* I said to myself as I pulled the bag close to me and put the lock in my pocket. The only thing left to do now was to safely get back to the car. I dashed back out into the parking lot, never turning to look back.

"Girl, what took you so long?" Tracy asked, as I slid back into her backseat.

"Don't even ask. Let's get the hell out of here."

"*With pleasure!*" Tracy said, as she drove off.

6

"Shit ain't so bad, just a little messed up that's all. 'Least they ain't demolish the place. You know, no holes in the walls or anything like that. Could be a lot worse," Malcolm tried to reassure me.

"Yeah... that's easy for you to say, though. You never saw what it looked like in there before any of this happened," I said.

"Believe me, sweetheart, I've seen my share of raids and know just how bad they can get. One thing for sure, two things for certain: them sheisty mother-fuckers went in there searchin' and probably left with a whole lot more than what they came with."

"Yeah, I know. That's what's worrying me."

"Yeah, well, ain't no sense in worryin' about it now. Let me do all the worrying for you. Shit will re-veal itself in time. Till then, just be cool and let me figure some things out."

"Hmm... all right," I said and exhaled.

"I'll check on you a little later. Just keep the keys in case you need them."

"Okay... thank you."

"Don't mention it."

I ended my call with my dear old friend and reclined my seat back. Good ole Malcolm. No matter what, he always came through in the ninth inning. After dark, he and I went back up to the apartment to assess the damages. With the yellow tape and crooked cops no longer in sight, the parking lot appeared innocent and untainted by wrongdoings or evildoers. In fact, other than the black dusting powder smeared across my front door, the previous night's events seemed a mere figment of my imagination. The inside, however, told a whole different story.

In darkness I fingered my way through clutter, going straight to obvious spots that could've housed any important items. Yet, I continuously came up empty-handed. My fears grew as my suspicions were now confirmed: the safes, the money, and even some of our collectibles were all gone. The only real valuables left were the cars parked outside and a few pieces of jewelry buried beneath all the mess. Yeah, Malcolm may have seen worst, but my gut told me *I hadn't* seen the worst of it yet. This I knew as soon as the gum-smacking, bad weave-having, black lip liner-wearing, young chick working the hospital's security desk, denied me visitation to see Mekhi. Her words, *"Family members only,"* echoed in my head as I politely turned to leave. On my way out, I thought to myself, *Bitch just mad cause she ugly.* But she needed not worry; I wanted no trouble. What I did want was for Mekhi's, "family members" to get the facts from me before any rumors started circulating about all that had taken place. So I tried reaching out to them, but then quickly had a change of heart once they started talking that ownership bullshit. Whatever reason they felt entitled to any money, cars, jewels, and furniture left behind from the raid was beyond me. Those greedy vultures seemed more focused on what we had, than how we were. Not one of them offered me any type of comfort and so I left wondering why I had even tried in the first place. Comfort, I was learning, was something I would need to seek out for myself. And sitting behind my windows' tint provided just that.

My quest to be soothed led me to park at this playground and sit behind the wheel of my Range Rover playing back the day's events. Here I could pretend that things were back to normal instead of watching them spiral out of my control. Hours before, this place had been lit up with children. But as daylight savings time kicked in, the children all disappeared and took off to wherever they found their security. Now the moving swings stood still and the slippery sliding boards seemed cold. But, still I sat, thinking about my man and secretly wishing I had my own secure place to run off to.

"Oh, what I wouldn't give to fall back into routine right now. Just what am I suppose to do now?" I said out loud as I gazed out the window.

Malcolm had been kind enough to let me park the rest of our cars on one of his lots and he had even given me a key to one of his vacant properties, but I wasn't ready to be alone. So where to now? If my parents were still living, there would be no question where I would go. But since their deaths, the only other person who offered a sense of stability and security (at least in my eyes) was Mekhi. Of course there were other family members and friends, but me and my high-profile relationship had long before been alienated from both worlds.

Ironically, the one place I knew I could go was the one place I didn't want to go: my good ole Bible-preachin', know-it-all, saved and sanctified grandmother's house. There I knew I was always welcome but I just didn't always feel like listening to her daily sermons.

"Well, here goes nothin'," I said out loud as I dialed her number.

"Praise God," she answered.

"Hey, Ma… what's going on over there?"

"Who is this?" she jokingly asked.

"Come on, Ma... you know who this is. It's me, your one and only grandchild."

"Well, howdy... I thought I did somethin' wrong to you. Ain't known whether you was living or dead."

"MMMAAA... why would you say something like that?"

" 'Cause you stopped taking my phone calls, that's why."

"No, I didn't. I just called you the other day," I lied.

"Oh, come on, chile. I ain't heard from you in a month of Sundays. It's good to hear you still breathin', though. What's going on over there that you couldn't pick up the phone and check on your good ole' grandma?"

"Well... ah... I was getting ready to ...um... 'cause I was... um... I ..."

"Well, ain't no sense in dragging it out over the phone. Won't you come on over and spend a little time with this old lady? I ain't the big bad wolf. I ain't the one that's gonna bite you," she said and laughed.

"Okay, I'm on my way."

"Now I know I must be talkin' to somebody else's grandchild. I ain't never got that quick of a response out of you."

"Well... I was just... ah... about..."

"...chile, you just get your butt on over here. You ain't gotta do no whole bunch of explaining to me. Just be careful and make sure you got that seatbelt on and I'll be right here waitin' for you when you get here. Okay?"

"All right, Ma. I'll see you then."

Well Gizelle, you done done it now... you done gone and opened up them gates and you know how she is. What you gonna do now? a little voice inside of me asked.

"I don't know, but I guess I can start by combing my hair," I said while pulling the visor down to check myself out in the mirror. I pulled my long black strands up into a loose bun before starting the truck. Thank goodness for Daddy--his deeply mixed roots saved me from a bad hair day on many occasions. Going in front of Grandma, I needed to pull off an innocent look because she could always read through any bullshit that was going on with me.

I reached behind my seat to make sure my black bag was still there because without it, I would really be up shit's creek. Right now, I needed to get out of this truck, collect my thoughts, and empty the contents of my bag. My grandmother's house would be just the place to do it.

I was dazed at a red light wondering what embellished truths I would tell her when my voicemail indicator went off.

That's funny, I didn't even hear the phone ring, I thought to myself as I dialed in to check the message.

"O'la, chica. You not wanna come out to play hide and seek? This my last night here," Yasmine's seductive voice teased.

Shit! I didn't know what it was about this woman that instantly got me wet. As I attempted to delete her message she left another one.

"Mmmm... just like that, Papi... ahhh... nn-nooo... I sorry... she say she comin'...nnooo... I promise... ahhh ...mmm don't stop... don't stop... ahhh."

Hearing her moan had me ready to ram my car into the person in front of me. They had started the show without me and as I listened to her take every inch of what Quazi had to offer, my inner thighs became moist in *preparation* and my pussy walls became tight with *anticipation*. I had to get over there. If I didn't go now, when would I get another chance to lose myself in the moment? Besides, what would be the harm if it were just this one last time?

I was trying my best to rationalize things out to benefit me, when I pulled in front of my grandmother's house. Judging from the familiar cars parked outside, she was hosting one of her famous card games. It was a scene I was all too accustomed to seeing while growing up there. "Good," I thought to myself, "at least she will be preoccupied while I attempt to get occupied elsewhere." I ran inside and spoke to everyone before heading upstairs to freshen up.

"Baby, you goin' somewhere?" she asked as I departed from the bathroom and made my way towards the front door.

"Yeah, Ma... I'll be back a little later. I got a few errands to run."

"Okay, well make sure you got your house keys just in case I'm sleep when you get back."

"Okay," I replied, as I double-checked my key ring and tossed my black bag over my shoulder. I was in too much of a hurry to check it so I'd decided to take it with me. Right then I only had one thing on my mind. Better yet, make that three: Me, him, and her!

7

The energy of B-more was alive and pumping throughout the downtown crowds of Saturday evening partygoers. Everywhere I turned there were people laughing and engulfed in one another's company. Boy was I glad I had decided to switch up cars. I had parked my loud-ass flashy truck, thinking that it would've definitely brought unwanted attention my way. Right then I just wanted to blend in with the crowd, not create a distraction. If nothing else, the windows tint on the five-year-old '97 Accord would give me all the privacy I needed. I was just within a few blocks of Quazi's condo when I decided to pull over and give him a call.

"Hey, I'm heading your way. I should be there in less than fifteen minutes," I said to the voice on the opposite end of the phone.

"You have to *find us*; the door open for you," Yasmine sang out before ending the call. I laughed to myself. From her tone I could tell she was more than a little tipsy.

I glanced around the strip mall lot I had pulled into; it too, was crowded with people intertwined in different scenarios of social gatherings. But, since none of them seemed to be paying me any mind, I pulled out my black bag and started removing its contents. A few undergarments, some toiletries, makeup, comb, brush, and toothpaste were all there just as I had placed them. But there was something beyond the surface which also needed to be emptied out. Section by section and stack by stack, I made my way to the bottom of the bag and was slowly able to see what had taken me years to build.

In front of me was a year's worth of unspent cashed checks. I had stashed the money, *my money*, away for a rainy day. And right now my forecast predictions called for hailing winds and pouring rains! There had to be close to $100,000 there, easy, all in mostly large bills.

No matter what happens, this should hold me over for a minute. I thought to myself as I placed everything back in the bag and continued on my way.

I promised myself that I would be done after I got this last rendezvous out of my system. I would simply focus all of my energy and attention on my man. Hell, if we make it through this one, I'll just tell him about my preferences and maybe we can create our own fantasies together. I pulled into Quazi's parking lot and squeezed in between a new convertible Benz and a Range Rover that looked similar to mine. I oiled my body down before changing into a trench and a pair of 4 inch, red bottoms I had in the trunk.

"All set?" I asked the person starring back at me through the mirror. I paused long enough to acknowledge the gut feeling I had telling me to turn around. But how could I when my body was screaming out for an orgasm? I needed this to loosen me up. Perhaps then, I would be better equipped to deal with any drama that was slowly brewing. So, against my better judgment, I shook away the feeling and continued on my way.

The elevator let me off at Quazi's penthouse and as I went to knock on the door, I noticed that Yasmine wasn't lying--the door was unlocked and slightly open. A pile of rose petals greeted me at the front door and invited me into the dim light.

"Hello... Hello... Is anyone here...?" I called out. When I didn't receive a response, I followed the scent of vanilla escaping from the huge crème candles illuminating the open space ahead of me. The sound of Maxwell's melodic tunes embraced me while ushering me further along into the enticing suite. I was half-way down the hall when I was suddenly grabbed from behind. I gasped as someone put one arm around my neck and the other around my waist.

"I thought you never show up. You keep us waiting, now you're it," Yasmine seductively whispered while tracing the outside of my ear with her tongue. I turned around just in time to catch a glimpse of her naked round ass before she disappeared into the huge open space of the converted warehouse.

"Giizzellllle, Gizzellle, my love. Where are you?" the charming masculine voice called out from above. I took off my coat and heels so that I could jump in and play.

"Come out, come out, wherever you are," I purred as I sensuously made my way up the marble spiral staircase. I checked the jacuzzi first, but only found bubbles, a pair of floating thongs, and two empty wine glasses.

"I guess I'll have to play with myself," I teased as I entered the master suite. Still, there was no sign of either one of them.

"Hellloooo? Why doesn't anyone wanna play with me?" I said right before sliding down a pole to get back downstairs.

"BOO!" Yasmine yelled, as she popped out of nowhere, squirting whipped cream in the air.

"Bitch, you scared the shit out of me," I tantalizingly whispered as I pulled her close to me.

"I sorry, chica. I make it up to you," she said and began to lick the cream from my nipples. I took the can from her and started to squirt my own dessert over her body.

"Now, now. Is that any way to treat a guest?" I asked, as I threw my tongue down her throat while starting a slow grind with her body.

"Mmmm... ahh," she moaned as I slid my hands between her thighs and fingered through her lips.

"You dun waste no time, eh?" Quazi called out from the loft.

"What you expect?" I said while tracing one of Yasmines nipples with my tongue. I took turns gently biting each one before popping the plump of each breast into my mouth. I then slid down and rested my head between her thighs before teasing her lips. With my tongue, I traced the outside of her pussy before diving into the house of her wetness.

"Ay, ya, ya Mami', no... no... ahhh..." she screamed out in passion while trying to guide my tongue towards the right spot. In and out, up and down, round and round, my tongue explored before coming back up to share the taste with her.

"Mmmm... now I have something for you," she said right before going down to return the favor.

"Ahhh... just like that Mami', don't stop..." I threw my head back and screamed out in pleasure. I grabbed one of the candles and slowly began to pour the melted wax down her back. We were having so much fun that I totally forgot about Quazi until I looked up and saw him making his way down to us.

"Care to join?" I asked.

"Tought you'd never ask. Now where ya been, to keep me waitin' 'round like dis eh?" he growled.

There was something familiar yet distant in his eyes that made him look a little different standing there in the darkness. I didn't know what it was, but it gave me a strange sense that I shouldn't be there. I shook the feeling and pushed the thought to the back of my head, along with everything else.

I turned from Yasmine to embrace him and noticed that he had one crutch under his arm. But before I could say anything, he was on his knees doing what he did best.

"Mmm," I moaned as the moisture of his tongue began to go to work on me. Yasmine grabbed me from behind, planted her plump breasts on my back and started to play with mine. There I stood helplessly captured in their eroticism.

Before I knew it, we were back upstairs and Quazi was spreading my legs apart, pushing himself deep inside of me. He seemed to be a little bigger than I remembered, which caused discomfort until Yasmine came over to have a turn. She climbed on top of me and folded her legs, scissor style, within mine.

"Ahh, Yasmineeee... no... ahhhh...wait...you nasty bitch, stop!" I screamed out and smacked her ass.

"Ahhh... no... don't beat me... ahh... I do it better... *you like that Mami'...huh... you like it?"* she said as she started a fast grind.

I looked up and noticed Quazi sneaking up behind her with his dick in his hands. As he pulled her towards him, I squirmed my way to the bottom of the bed and again went to work on her. The more they moaned the more I threw myself into their world and out of mine. I let my tongue guide the way between the two of them until I knew Quazi could no longer take it. He pulled out of Yasmine and threw himself into my mouth.

"Uh, umm, take it from Daddy... AAAHHHH!" he yelled out, as he thrusted back once more before exploding.

I licked him over one last time before releasing him from my hold. I was having so much fun that I barely noticed the alarm going off in the background.

"No..." I said.

"Yes, Mami', yes." they both said while trying to lure me into another session.

"Nnnooo..." I said again.

"Yesss, oh yes!" Quazi screamed out.

"Nnnnooo, please God, *NNOOOOO!*" I said breaking away from their grasp.

"BEEP...BEEP...BEEP...*BEEP!*" The alarm continued.

"Oh my, God! SSSSHHHIIIIITTTTT! I GOTTA GO!" I shouted out and ran towards the stairs. I was in such a hurry that I missed the top step and fell head-first down the rest. I got a big lip, a busted knee, and a bruised arm in my haste.

"Please, God no, oh NO...please...please...not this!" I said as I banged the elevator buttons in frustration. When I finally made it to the lot I ran towards my car like a mad woman. The closer I got, the clearer the sound became. I only prayed it was a false alarm.

Panting and heaving, I swung my car door open and soon realized that my prayers had fallen on deaf ears. Hysterically, I searched the car, but in the end all I found was a flashlight and a couple of mints.

"*FUCK! FFFUUUCCCK!* OH GOD, PLEASE NOT THIS! WHY? WHY ME...WHY THIS?" I screamed out into the cold night air. I had become so involved in my argument with God that I hadn't bothered to notice just how much of a scene I was creating.

"Honey, do you want me to call for help...a doctor maybe...is everything okay?" someone came up to me and asked.

"Oh, now you're concerned! Where was all the goddamn concern when I was getting ripped the fuck off? *NO* everything is not okay, and *NO* a doctor won't be able to fix this shit, but what do you *care*?" I said as I wiped my face and fastened the belt on my trench. The older white woman quietly walked back to her friends, shrugging her shoulders.

Confused and dazed, I climbed into my car and started making my way to my apartment. I was about halfway there when it dawned on me that I couldn't go there, it was no longer my home. I U-turned and started back towards my grandmother's house, crying all the way.

8

What in the hell was going on? First Mekhi and now *this*. What had I done to deserve this? I had only indulged in a few moments of pleasure and in an instant, my entire life savings had been snatched away from me. $100,000 gone just like that. What was I supposed to do now? I thought about calling Malcolm. Hell, I even thought about telling Mekhi. But what would I say, "Hey, I was a little stressed and needed to release some steam, so I met up with an island friend and his girl for a late night freak show. While they took turns eating my pussy, somebody stole my shit?" That would surely land me in a hospital room next to Mekhi's. No, this one I would have to take on the chin no matter how much it was eating me up inside. I left Quazi's and drove around for hours trying to make sense of it all. For the life of me, I just didn't get it.

All I wanna do now is sleep, I thought to myself as I crept up my grandmother's stairs and settled into one of her spare rooms. With all the card players gone, the house was left quiet, dark and empty--much like I felt on the inside. Physically exhausted and emotionally drained, I tearfully drifted off and when I opened my eyes my mother stood before me glowing; a perfect angelic vision in all white.

"MA...MA!" I tried calling out. But when no sound escaped my mouth, I tried yelling again, "MA...MMAAA," and still nothing.

There we stood, suspended in midair, silently embracing one another. Everything around me seemed unfamiliar except for her. I was so glad to be there with her. There was so much I had to say. I started again, "Ma, guess what? Wait till you hear what just happened to me. I have *sssooo* much to tell you," I said, while trying to loosen her grip. I wanted to see her face but I couldn't because of the way she was holding me. I wiggled and squirmed, then pulled and tugged, but it was of no use--she wouldn't let me go.

A harsh wind blew past that was so strong, I was sure it would have carried me away if it had not of been for her embrace. Quietly, I started to cry. There was so much I wanted to say to her; so much I had to fill her in on, but all I could do right then was stand still and be held. I knew she cared about me and what

I was going through, but why wouldn't she let me go?

The next morning, I got up extra early with plans of seeing my man. Things were starting to go very wrong very fast and I was counting on him to make them right again. I was also trying my best to avoid my grandmother and thought I had succeeded until I went to grab my coat and heard her say, "Got in kind of late last night didn't you... and now up *mighty* early... *some errands, huh*?"

"Shit," I silently mouthed as I slowly turned to face her. "Oh... good morning, Ma. I didn't know you were up yet."

"Yeah, I'm up. Been up ever since the detective left."

"Detective?" I asked in amazement.

"Yes, detective, chile, you heard me. Or is you hard of hearing now, too?"

"What did you tell him?" I nervously asked.

"What could I tell him? I don't know shit," my grandmother giggled. "Now is there somethin' *you* wanna tell me?"

"Well... I was gonna tell you last night, Ma, but you were playing cards when I got here," I said, as I slowly begin to rehash the grimy details of my weekend. I concluded by telling her that I had gone to see a friend last night for consoling and had been ripped off in the process. Purposely leaving out what type of consoling and just how much had been stolen from me. When I was done, I looked up to see her reaction. Up until then she had been sitting quietly, sipping her morning coffee.

"Well, you know the detective seems to think you're both in a lot of trouble. Whose name is on the lease, yours or his?"

"Mine...just mine."

"Do you know all that was in the apartment?"

"No...I mean I had some ideas, but no, not specifically."

"Have you been to see him yet?" she quietly asked.

"No. I tried yesterday, but they wouldn't let me in. I was gonna try again today."

"Now help me understand again...why you just now telling me all of this?"

"Well...when I came in last night you were playing cards...so..."

"So why didn't you pull me to the side, Zella? You know you can't just be running 'round here doing what you wanna do when you wanna do it, 'specially with so much going on!"

"I know...I know," I said trying my best to wrap up what I knew was coming.

"No you don't, either, and that's the problem. You young'uns always thinkin' you the first to ever do shit. Don't you know in life, history just repeats itself? Now if you live long enough, sooner or later you'll find that out."

"Swooo," I huffed and rolled my eyes. I knew this was coming.

"You can huff and puff all you want to, but I'll tell you this... this is just the beginning of something much bigger for *you*. Now I'm sorry that you and Mekhi have to go through all of this, but trust me when I say, this has been a long time comin' and *He* don't make no mistakes. Now I've tried not to get involved in your business all these years, but I ain't no fool neither and I knew why you'd stay away. But you mark my word, He's trying to get your attention the best way He knows how. Now what *you* need to do is sit your hard-headed, fast ass down long enough to think about all *He's* trying to say to you."

"But Grandma, that ain't fair. You act like this is my fault, like I did something to deserve all of this," I said, in my defense.

"Chile, is that all you got from what I just said? I'm talkin' about the message *He's* trying to give *you, girl.* Things ain't always gonna be fair, honey. That's life. But you gotta learn how to play the hand that's dealt to you, baby. That's the only way you're gonna make it in this world. There's an old saying that goes, *'things turn out best for those who make the best out of the way things turn out.*' Now I know things ain't always been easy, 'specially with your mother and father being gone, but you're growing up now and with age comes both responsibility and accountability. Do you understand what I'm sayin' to you?"

"Yes... no... I think so."

My grandmother paused before continuing, "Gizelle, you gotta start being honest with yourself. But in order to do that, you have to know who you are and be at peace with your findings. Can you honestly say you know who you are?"

"Yeah, of course I do," I answered matter-of-factly.

"Who are you?" she snapped back.

"I'm Gizelle," I said and laughed a little.

"And who is she? Have you ever really given yourself a chance to know who she is?"

"Yeah... what do you mean?"

"I don't think you have, baby, and that's one question I can't answer for you. But what I can do is share some of my wisdom to try and prevent you from the pain of some hard lessons. You can't run from life, baby, and you can't hide from *you* either. The sooner you realize that, the better off you'll be. Now, I'm gonna lie down. I gotta absorb all that you've just said and more of what you didn't," my grandmother said, giving me a knowing look as she disappeared from the room with her Bible.

I hauled ass towards the front door and breathed a huge sigh of relief once inside my car. I knew somebody would come to question me, but I didn't think it would be this soon. I hadn't even met with an attorney yet and I was in no rush to. I would talk to all of them in due time and on my time. Right now I needed to get some other things squared away first. Judging from the conversation I had just had, finding another place to stay was at the top of my list. That I would work on immediately after I came from seeing Mekhi.

I stopped to grab some "Get Well" balloons and decided to call Mekhi's best friend in the process. I knew he would inform me of anything I needed to tell Mekhi.

"Hello."

"Hey, Jeremy, this is Gizelle. How's everything going?"

"Hey, Gizelle, I was just thinking about you. I want to talk some things over with you. Have you seen Mekhi yet?"

"No, I tried to yesterday, but they wouldn't let me in. I figured if I go now things would probably be a little bit more relaxed. I can meet you first though, if you want me too."

"Yeah, Tracy told me they wouldn't let you in. No, you go ahead and I'll meet up with you a little later.

Just be careful going back down there, you know they got people watching him."

"Yeah, I figured as much. Is there anything you can tell me over the phone?"

"Naw, I'd rather talk to you in person."

"Okay, I'll call you later then."

"Okay. He's up on the 8th floor, room 138."

"Thanks, Jeremy. Have you been to see him yet?"

"No... not yet... we'll talk a little more, later."

"Okay, talk to you then."

"All right."

This time I didn't bother stopping by the hospital's security desk. Instead, I headed straight towards the elevators. And sure as hell, off to the right and directly outside of Mekhi's room, was a guard.

"Shit!" I said to myself as I glanced around to see if there was more than one guard, or if I recognized this one from my apartment the other night. He didn't look familiar, so I walked right up to him with the best little girl's voice I could muster and said, "Excuse me, sir, is this Mekhi Stevenson's room?"

"Yes, but only family members are allowed in. Are you related?" the senior gentleman asked.

"Yes, sir," I lied, thinking back to the last time I was here.

"Do you have an ID I can see?"

"Shoot! I was rushing and must have left it in the house.

"Then I'm sorry, young lady, I can't let you in."

"Can I please just give him these balloons, sir?"

"I'm afraid not without..."

"Oh please, sir! I just wanna give him these balloons and let him know that I'm praying for him. I promise not to be long," I pleaded.

"I really can't ..."

"Two minutes. I promise not to take more than two minutes, I swear."

The guard looked me over once more before reluctantly saying, "You've got two minutes young lady, but you have to sign this form before I let you go in."

"Okay, thank you so much, sir. I really appreciate it," I said as I quickly glanced over the sheet he handed me to sign. There was a Tiffany, a Samantha, a Brooke, a Keisha, a Tammy, an Ashley, a Bridgette, and some other names listed before mine. I didn't know how they managed to get in because I knew they weren't all family members. Instantly, I caught an attitude. *This shit is crazy. It don't ever stop with him,* I thought to myself, as I made my way into his room.

"Hey, I see you had some visitors. Is that why I couldn't get in the other day?" I greeted him.

"Yeah, just a few family members… friends… business affiliates, you know how that go. I was waiting for you. What's going on out there now?"

"I'm not really sure, my grandmother told me a detective came past looking for me, but she sent him away. I just talked to Jeremy, but he said he'd rather talk in person. How're you feeling?" I said, trying my best to keep my mind off of the list of names I had just seen.

"Better now. The Doctor says I'll probably have a slight limp, but I'll live. I was worried as shit about you. I called my lawyer as soon as I got word about the raid. He's looking into everything. Where are you staying?"

"With my grandmother."

"What happened to your lip?" Mekhi asked, catching me completely off guard.

"You know how clumsy I am. I ran into the door yesterday after they okay'd me to leave," I lied.

"You gotta be a little more careful baby. You going back out to the apartment?"

"Only to clean and move things out. I gotta get a storage unit first, and Jeremy wants me to meet up with him once I leave here."

"Check the place by the highway, bin 519… password same as the voicemail out at the house. The key should be on the side of the basket in the bedroom and don't worry about Jeremy, I'll talk to him later. Just make sure you get my stuff from the bin," Mekhi whispered to me. I nodded my head in acknowledgement. This was the first time I had ever heard of any storage unit. I looked out at the guard and noticed him glancing down at his watch.

"I gotta go, he only gave me two minutes. I still got my cell, though. Just call me when you can."

"Okay, I will. I love you."

"I love you, too," I said, leaning in to kiss him goodbye.

There was something about the way he mentioned the storage unit that had me intrigued. I only hoped no one got to whatever it was before I had a chance to.

A few hours passed since I saw Mekhi and I decided it best not to go back up to the apartment. Because it was Sunday, I was sure that all of my neighbors were home and I really didn't feel like being under their watchful eyes. Instead, I mapped out a plan for the next day and went to bed early complaining of a stomachache. It was all that I could think of to keep my grandmother from another lecturing session. I was lying in bed watching television, when I saw Tracy's number pop up on my cell.

"Hello," I answered, acting as if I had just been awakened.

"Hey, girl, you 'sleep?" Tracy asked, as I positioned the phone on my shoulder.

"No, just got in bed, though."

"You in bed early, you feeling okay?"

"Yeah, I guess, just kind of drained. I guess everything is taking its toll on me."

"Yeah, I can imagine. Look, I called to see if you were out late last night 'cause one of my girlfriends swore me up and down that she saw you."

"I don't know any of your girlfriends. Why does she think she saw me?" I nervously asked.

"Girl, you know Baltimore ain't but so big and everybody knows them cars. She was with her boyfriend and I think he knows Mekhi."

"What did they say?" I asked, trying my best to sound nonchalant. The last thing I needed was for last night to get out.

"She said they were behind you at a light, but you sped off. I told her it wasn't you, though."

"I came in and went to bed early last night. I did stop and grab something to eat, though. Maybe they saw me then," I said, trying to throw her off.

"I don't know, maybe. She said this was downtown by the water. You know, where some of them ballers live? Well look, I'm not gonna hold you up. I was just checking on you. Just call me when you're feeling better," Tracy finally said.

"Okay, I will."

Shit, it had to be me that they saw, but how much did they see? Fuck! I needed to find out who this couple was, but right now wasn't the time. I had a big day ahead of me and would need all of my energy to focus on the tasks at hand.

9

A blistery November chill seeped through a cracked window and woke me up much earlier than I anticipated. If I'd forgotten before that winter was right around the corner, I sure as hell remembered now. The cold air filled the room and seemed to set the tone, as I got up and called out sick from work. I couldn't go back in yet. Right now, I didn't feel like dealing with anybody's business but my own. Besides, judging from the vibe Mekhi had given me, I was the only one who could tie up the few loose ends we had hanging around.

As I climbed in my car and got started with my day, I couldn't help but notice the serene picturesque vision forming behind me. The fallen autumn leaves scattered throughout the streets had set the background as the sun slowly began to rise. It was nature at its best and it was beautiful. I couldn't remember the last time I had been up early enough to witness

Mother Nature at her core, but here I was making my way back up to the apartment. I was seemingly carefree on the outside and nervous as hell on the inside. This would be my first trip back there alone and I didn't want any unexpected visitors.

I drove past it twice before deciding to go in. Once inside, a feeling of desecration and disgust crept all over me. The whole apartment was in disarray and practically everything we owned had been disturbed and tossed about somewhere. Pictures had been pulled from the walls, furniture had been moved, and trash cans were flooded with donut boxes and coffee cups. *Just how long were them crooked bastards in here?* I wondered, as I tried my best to stay focused.

At first sight, locating anybody's basket and key seemed impossible. But I was on a mission, and as I began to clean, things slowly started taking shape. Pretty soon hours had passed and things looked halfway normal again. Beneath it all, the basket Mekhi had spoken about finally emerged.

I sat down for the first time since I had been there and fingered through the wicker design to locate the key.

"YES!" I exclaimed as soon as my finger touched the cold metal. The only thing left was to find out exactly what it would unlock. I finished cleaning, bagged a few items to take with me, and jumped back on the highway. It took me all of fifteen minutes to locate the storage building and right then, I anxiously stood outside of bin 519. I pulled the small key from my bra and examined the two locks that were guarding the unit. I only had one key and couldn't remember whether Mekhi had said anything about two. If he did, I sure as hell didn't see them.

"Guess I'll soon find out," I said as I unlocked the first lock and prayed hard that the second one would be so easy. Somebody must've been listening because that *one* key fit both locks.

I stepped inside of the small storage space and looked around. One side held stacked totes, and aligned on the other side were weights and shoe boxes.

"Looks like this won't be as quick as I thought," I said, as I got straight to work.

I knew my man well enough to know that I had to be searching for something of dire importance; otherwise he wouldn't have mentioned this place at all. I searched and searched, but for the most part didn't find anything of significance. I was digging through the last tote when my hand hit something hard buried beneath a tall stack of jeans.

I dug a little deeper and tried to pull it through, but it was way too heavy to lift. I would have to empty the tote in order to reach it. I started removing item by item, when the strong whiff of moth balls hit me.

"Woo. I see I wasn't the only one who kept a secret stash," I said to myself, as my eyes focused on the money in front of me. I pulled out what I estimated to be triple of what I had previously saved for myself. I knew Mekhi kept money in the house, in different bank accounts, and in safe deposit boxes. But I would've never guessed that he had this much stashed away somewhere else. What was I suppose to do with it? I couldn't leave it here and if I took it with me, where would I put it? Not wanting to go back to Grandma's, I still had no real place to stay.

"Beeeeep… bbbbeeeeep beep beep beep beep." My cell went off, scaring the hell out of me.

"Right on time," I said, looking at Malcolm's number on the caller ID. Little did he know, he had just answered my question.

"Well, hello there!" I cheerfully answered.

"Where the hell have you been?" he demanded.

"Some greeting. Have you missed me, baby?" I said and giggled.

"Why haven't you called to let me know what's going on with you?"

"What do you mean, what's going on with me?" I joked.

"Don't play with me. You don't take my calls, you don't text. And you moved the cars from the lot. What's going on over there in your head, doll? I need to see you."

"You do know I'm grown, right? Twenty-six years old to be exact. You trying to keep tabs on me or something?" I teasingly asked.

"I'm serious, Gizelle. I've been calling you over the past few days but kept getting your voicemail."

"Did you leave a message? You didn't call if you didn't leave a message."

"Stop playing with me. This *is* my goddamn message!"

"Okay... calm down, geez. I'm still breathing. I had some things I needed to take care of, but I'm headed your way right now. Just tell me where you are."

"How are you headed my way, if I gotta tell you where I am?"

"Oh, so now you got jokes? You know what I mean."

"I'm house-sitting for my mother. Do you remember how to get here?" Malcolm asked.

"Yup, I'm on my way now. Are you alone?"

"Who else would be here? Of course I'm alone."

"Okay, smart ass. I was just checking. Give me about 15 minutes."

"You got 10."

Good ole Malcolm saves the day again. I had forgotten all about the spare key he had given me earlier on. I just hoped it wasn't too late to make good use of it. I bagged up about half of the money to take out with me when my phone started to beep again. I looked down at the caller ID this time and felt less enthused. It was my grandmother and I didn't bother to answer. I wasn't about to let her spoil my mood with all of her ideologies about life. Things were much different when she was growing up so why she felt like I was repeating some type of history lesson, was beyond me. She just didn't get it and besides, things were halfway back on track now. This money would take care of half of my problems and Mekhi had a lawyer that would take care of the other half. All I had to do was lay low until he came home and who better to help me with that than good ole Malcolm?

10

"Damn, he knew I was on my way over here. Where in the hell could he have gone so fast?" I said as I walked away from Malcolm's mother's house.

"You're so fast. Where are you going?" Malcolm said swinging the front door open.

"I was about to leave. You know I don't like waiting around. Come help me with these bags."

"Bags? I said *I* was house-sitting, not *you*," he joked.

"Boy, whateva'. I don't wanna tempt nobody and leave 'em out here."

"What's in it for me?" he asked, biting down on his bottom lip. He was just testing me now because he knew that shit turned me on.

"I don't know. How much time we got?" I teased.

"As long as it'll take."

"Take these," I smiled, while handing over some bags. "Is that why you wanted to see me so bad?"

"Could be. What's with all the bags?"

"I just came from cleaning the apartment."

"Oh. Come here and let me take a look at you. It ain't like you to not keep in touch. What's really been going on in that head of yours?"

"Aawww, poor thing. Have you really been that worried? I'm sorry sweetheart, I wasn't thinking. Tell me how to make it up to you," I joked as I slowly walked over and brushed up against him.

"Come on now, leave that alone. All jokes aside, Gizelle, I was starting to think somebody came and snatched you up," Malcolm said as we walked into his mother's huge single family dwelling. The walls were white and the décor was very upscale. Colorful, contemporary Italian pieces were spread out everywhere. The place was flawless and Malcolm wasn't looking too bad either. His dark, chocolate skin appeared unblemished and there wasn't an ounce of fat on his muscular frame.

"Well, a detective did come by the other day, but my grandmother chased him away. What's up? It ain't like *you* to be so serious. You must've heard something," I said.

"You haven't been reading the paper?" he asked.

"No, is there a manhunt out for me or something?" I nervously asked.

"You tell me. Huh, see for yourself," he said, while handing over the police blotter section of our town's paper.

The headlines read: "County police stumble on drug lord during attempted robbery...guns... kilos...hoards of money...possible federal charges... suspect currently being held..."

"They must have just taken him into custody because I was just with him yesterday," I said as I skimmed over the rest of the article.

"Oh, so you have seen him?" Malcolm questioned.

"Yeah, but he was still in the hospital when I did. And even then, the guard only gave me a few minutes. Them rotten bastards. How can they do this when we were the ones who called for help? They weren't even supposed to be in the apartment in the first place. Not to mention, they didn't say one word about the boys who shot him," I said while slamming the article on the table. I was pissed. I felt like everybody was missing the goddamn point but me. If they didn't have just cause to be in my apartment, why should it matter what was found?

"I hear you babe, but you already know how petty them motherfuckers can be, especially when they see a nigga' bringin' in more than what they are. If you think they play fair, you're crazy. It's the story of our lives and the reality of it all is that Christmas just came early for them rotten bitches. What did your boyfriend have to say about all of this? Does he know what's going on out here?"

"Yeah, he knows. He may not have all the facts, but he knows. He said he's got his lawyer looking into things."

"Who he workin' with?"

"I don't know, but I'm supposed to meet up with him later this week."

"Well, there you have it. I just wanted to make sure you were okay and that you were watchin' out for yourself. I started to put out an APB on you," Malcolm joked.

"Yeah, right," I said, barely listening. I was still taking in all that I'd just read.

"I'm serious. You know this town and you know how fast news travels. You gotta watch yourself. You don't want nobody comin' after you, thinking you sittin' on something that you're not."

"Too late," I said, thinking back to my night with Quazi.

"What do you mean?" Malcolm looked at me and asked.

"The other night somebody broke into my car. Why do you think I brought all this stuff in here with me?"

"Seriously? Damn, baby."

"I know."

"That's the shit I'm talkin' 'bout though, you gotta' be careful. Where you stayin'?"

"Well, I was staying at my grandmother's, but I'm wondering if the spare key offer was still good with you. I don't feel like dealing with her stuff right now."

"I feel you, especially if the detectives have already started questioning her. Listen, why don't you just camp out here with me? My mother will be gone for another two weeks, maybe even longer; that way I can keep an eye on you."

"I don't know, you might try and take advantage of me," I said with a smirk.

"Don't you mean that the other way around?" Malcolm asked and smiled. "Come on, let's go. Come take a ride with me. You probably could use some fresh air anyway," Malcolm said, while grabbing his keys from the counter.

"Where are we going?" I asked while trailing behind.

"Just come on. Ain't like you got somewhere else to go," he said as he opened the hallway door leading to the garage.

"I thought you didn't like driving this fancy car anymore," I said as I got into the passenger's side of his BMW 750.

"I don't. I only pull it out for royalty and special occasions. You just happen to be a little of both," he said, and winked as we took off down the block.

It had been close to a year since Malcolm and I had hung out together. But after the day we had just had, I was convinced that no amount of time or distance would ever alter my feelings for this man. Something about his effortless way of uncomplicating things made it easy to lose sight of my world and get caught up in his. Or maybe it was his spur of the moment ideas of fun. Today he had practically lured me into a much-needed escapade, which went from sightseeing in Annapolis, to shopping in Georgetown, dinner in Virginia, and now back to his mother's house. It was getting late and not only had I lost all track of time, but I had also lost all consciousness of my dilemmas.

"Thank you, sweetheart. You were right, the fresh air did do some good," I said as we walked through his mother's kitchen and into her living room. "I owe you one for that," I said as I planted a big kiss on his cheek.

"Anytime babe, anytime. But please don't start counting now," he laughed, as he threw himself back on the enormous crème-colored leather sofa.

"Okay, I'll have to remember that," I said plopping down beside him.

"Come here, you know I'm just playin' with you. I knew you needed something to take your mind off things. In fact, I know you like a book."

"I wouldn't go that far," I jokingly said before getting up to dig my Papi bear out from one of my bags.

"Shit, you crazy. I know you inside and out. What's with the bear though? That's new. You tryin' to keep him away? He ain't gonna bite, unless you want him to," Malcolm joked as he made mention of that glorious thing poking up between his legs.

"Ha, ha, very funny. It's my bear, no biggie."

"Obviously, I can see that much. Who gave it to you, your boyfriend?"

"You tell me, Mr. Know-It-All. You're the one who knows me like a book," I laughed and said.

"Okay, keep it to yourself then."

"I will. I'm just joking, Malcolm, geez. It's my Papi bear and no, my boyfriend didn't give it to me, my father did right before he died."

"Oh."

"I used to pull it out when I wanted to feel close to him, but lately I can't sleep without it."

"That's deep, sweetheart. I didn't know that."

" 'Cause you don't know everything about me. But that's okay, I love you just the same," I said, planting another kiss on his cheek.

"You're crazy. I still say I know you inside-out."

"You didn't know about my bear, but I'll give you another try. Go ahead doctor, what's my prognosis?" I said as I crossed my legs and laid back, pretending to be his patient. I could feel the earlier glasses of wine, from dinner, starting to kick in.

"You're a young woman."

"Duh! Obviously," I said, swinging a pillow over his head.

"Hold up, you ain't let me finish yet," he said, throwing the pillow back.

"You're a young, beautiful woman in search of love."

"What?!" I said and laughed.

"I'm serious. Deep down, you wanna feel loved, protected, and desired just like every other woman or every other person, I might say."

"Yes, you might," I said and smiled.

"The catch is learning how to express it," Malcolm said and winked.

"Okay. So tell me, *Doctor*, since you seem to have all the answers; is that something you think you can help me with?" I said, while climbing up on his lap.

"I can help you with a lot of things, but you know that already don't you?" he said, as he grabbed my hips.

"I do. Perhaps then, a better question would be: How do you plan to help me? You got a formula you give every other woman such as myself?" I asked, as I slipped my shirt over my head exposing my bare breasts.

"Damn, baby, that's how you feel? I've got more than a formula to give," Malcolm said as he began to kiss on my neck.

"Oh, yeah? What else you got?"

"Everything you need."

"And what is it that I need?"

"A little bit of this," he said, while gently biting one of my nipples.

"A little bit of that," he commented, while making his way over to the other. "And a whole lot of this."

Malcolm then positioned my bottom half on top of his shoulders and with his tongue, slowly began to trace down to my midsection while pretending to write something across the outside of my lips.

"Mmm. I've missed you sssooo much."

"I missed you too, baby. I forgot how good you taste."

"I wanna feel you move inside of me, Malcolm."

"You sure that's what you want?" he asked, as he slipped out of his pants.

"Yes, baby, I'm sure."

He delicately laid me down on top of a huge plush rug which was directly in front of a gigantic, rectangular floor-length mirror.

"You know what I want. I wanna watch you move. Can I watch you take this dick from daddy?" he asked, while turning me over.

"Yes, baby, just please put it in. I don't know how much longer I can wait."

"Tell me how bad you want it," he demanded from behind.

"I want it so bad, baby. I can't take it. Malcolm…" I pleaded as I backed up towards him.

"You gonna take it all?"

"Yes, baby, yes!"

"You promise?"

"Yes, I promise."

"Tell me it's mine."

"It's yours, baby. It's always gonna be yours."

"You sure about that?" Malcolm asked, before slipping the tip of his head in and then pulling it right back out.

"You ain't ready. You don't want it," he teased.

"I do Malcolm, I swear I do. Baby, please put it back in," I said as I reached down and tried to do it myself.

"*EEEECCCKKKK!*" came from the door behind us. We both looked up at our reflections, but neither one of us stopped. Whoever it was, was about to get a hardcore lesson in Fucking 101.

"Baby, what's that?" I finally asked.

"What's what?"

"CCCCLLLIIICCCKKKK," went the lock.

"That! What's that? I thought you said your mother was gone."

"She is. Why, you want me to stop?" he asked, while diving deeper inside of me.

"Malcolm, shit!"

"That's what I thought."

"Agh!" I screamed out, all the while feeling paralyzed in pure ecstasy.

I lifted my head and watched through the mirror as the front door slowly opened and only then did Malcolm answer, never missing a stroke, "*Mia.*"

I looked at him as I brought my hand back up to my mouth and licked my fingers.

"Mmmm… baby wait…"

"For what...I haven't done anything yet...I'm not gonna do anything you don't want me to do...stop... move your hand," Malcolm said while slapping my hand away. He massaged his dick once more before slipping it back in.

"...mmm...agh...Malcolm, baby...wait..."

"Wait, shit...you know how long I've been waiting for this. Shit! It's so fuckin' good, baby. Tell me it's good!"

"Malcolm...baby...it's..." I lifted up and whined.

"Lay back, I got you," he said, gently pushing me back down. I reached down again and tried to grab his dick.

"Stop. Let me do it. I know what you want I'ma give you exactly what you asked for..."

"Agh! No..."

"No, what? You want me to stop... huh?" he asked, as he continued to plunge deeper.

"No..."

"That's what I thought. Tell me it's good."

"Baby....mmmm...it's..." I moaned.

"Yes, baby, yes. Tell daddy what you want..." he said, as he bent down to kiss me.

"...more... baby... mmm... I want more... it's... it's my turn," I whispered while returning his kiss.

"Yes it is. What you got for me? Come here and tell daddy how you want it," he said, as he pulled out from Mia and turned to caress me.

"Mmm..." I lifted up and moaned.

"Naw... where you think you goin'? Stay right here," he said, while pushing me back down beside Mia. She turned over and climbed on top of me as Malcolm gripped my waist and glided in.

"Tell him it's good," Mia whispered, as she nibbled on my ear.

"It's good. It's so fuckin' good."

"You sure?"

"Yes, Mia. Fuck!"

"Oh, you so fuckin' nasty... do it, baby ...goddamn it's so wet!"

As Malcolm hovered above the two of us, continuing to stroke me on the inside and grind on Mia from the outside; the sensation of it all became too much to bear.

"No...I can't... I can't take it... agh!" I yelled out, and wrapped my legs around her tighter. Malcolm, stop, baby... you gonna make me...agh..."

"Let daddy feel it, oh shit! You nasty bitch... hold up... AGH!" Malcolm shouted, as he pushed Mia down harder on top of me. Unable to hold back any longer, Mia bit down on my neck and moaned as she let everything she had been holding inside free to run down my legs. Malcolm thrust back one last time before plunging all the way in.

"Woo! Damn, that shit was good. I gotta get you drunk more often," he said, right before collapsing beside us. I kissed him once more before closing my eyes and drifting off...

11

I sat there and cried and not once did he say a word; he only looked past me. The intensity and silence were unbearable.

"Say somethin', ANYTHING... JUST SAY SOME-THIN'!" I voicelessly demanded from my soul's core. The truth was, his expression said it all. No amount of words or gestures could ever soften the blow. I looked up once more as he continued to walk further away and a wave of emotions hit me.

What had just happened? I thought to myself, as I started to cry harder. I looked around, engulfed in the stillness which filled this moment, and only then did I realize that I didn't know where I was, how I had gotten there, or if any of it truly existed. The only thing I knew for certain was the overwhelming feeling in my heart.

When I subconsciously overheard my cell ringing to the tune of 50 Cent's new hit single, "In Da Club",

I opened my eyes and raised my seat. I must have dozed off while waiting for my doctor's office to open.

"How strange is that?" I said to myself, referring to the dream I had just had and the tears that were now running down my cheeks. For the life of me I couldn't remember what I had just been dreaming about. I only knew the feeling that came from it. It must have been something awfully close to my heart to have moved me to tears, especially for a dream. When the musical melody started again, I picked up my cell and saw that I had a text from Quazi and a missed call from my grandmother. The text read, "Can I see you this weekend? –Q."

"Hell no," I said to myself.

I had talked to him only once since that awful night just to see what type of excuse he would offer for not coming down to check on me. And just as I thought, it was lame. He claimed to be so out of it that he hadn't even noticed I was gone until the next morning. I hung up on his ass and had been rejecting his calls ever since. I was done with him. The whole ordeal had left a bad taste in my mouth and I was trying to forget that it had ever happened.

I figured I'd call my grandmother back after my appointment. For some reason, she had become a little more relaxed with her lectures lately. I guess after I pulled my little disappearing act a few weeks ago with Malcolm, she had realized just how wrong she was for coming down on me so hard. I was back at her house now. I had been staying there for the past two weeks trying to get things back in order.

My short stay with Malcolm had been fun, but boy was I paying for it. It felt like he had stretched me beyond what I was used to. I had even started doing a few Kegels to try and tighten things back up before Mekhi came home, but only he would be able to tell if they really worked. I was hoping like hell that they had, because he would be home tomorrow. That is, if Mr. Canallini came through as promised.

Mr. Jude Canallini was the attorney we had retained for the battle ahead of us. Mekhi claimed he would need someone vicious and that Mr. Canallini was the right man for the job. I didn't know how vicious he was, but if his prices were indicative of his abilities, then we had the best guy for the job. He wanted $25,000 to be retained, another $25,000 for his first court appearance, and yet another $25,000 for research. And we were nowhere near a final hearing. At this rate, we were running through Mekhi's stash quicker than an Olympic runner. Between attorney's fees, bills, and other miscellanea, half of what I took out of storage was damn near gone. And the authorities had frozen any and everything else.

It seemed like every day something new was being added to the equation and the effects of it all had begun to take their toll on me. I had become drained. The chore of juggling things around and setting up house here and there had me more than exhausted. I needed to relax and kick back in my own space, which I would be able to do tomorrow if things went as planned.

The plan was that Mekhi would call, I would go and pick him up, and then we would head straight to one of his properties. There we would stay until some of this shit had a chance to blow over.

I looked up and noticed the doors had finally opened to my primary care doctor's office. I got out of my car and looked at my reflection through the window. Today I was in rare form; talk about playing the role! I had on mismatched socks, my hair was tussled, my clothes hadn't been ironed, and I was walking with a slight limp. I just hoped my doctor would buy into it. I knew I was pushing it, but I needed him to grant me a little more sick time away from work.

"Good morning. I have an 8 o'clock appointment with Dr. Amir," I greeted the older woman behind the desk.

"Good morning. Ms. Sadiq, right?" she asked while looking down at the chart in front of her.

"Yes, that's correct."

"Great. Amy can you escort Ms. Sadiq back to the first room?" she asked the blonde, slender woman behind her.

"Sure. You can follow me."

She ushered me back into a small room before beginning her routine questions.

"So what brings you into our office today?" the soft-spoken nurse asked.

"Well, Dr. Amir told me to come back if my migraines didn't ease up."

"Gotcha. So the prescription didn't help any?"

"No, not really. It actually seems like it made them worse," I lied, as I watched her jot down some notes.

"Have you tried isolating them to a certain time of day or month, maybe?"

"Yes, I did at first. But all I noticed was that they sporadically come and when they do they stop me dead in my tracks."

"You poor thing. My sister use to suffer from migraines when we were younger so I know how agonizing they can be. I'll let the doctor know what you've said. Are there any other issues he should know about?"

"No, I think that about covers it," I said as I started to squint. I needed to make sure I put on a good show.

"Okay. Well, he'll be here in just a moment." she said, as she started to leave the room. "Oh, I almost forgot," she turned around and said. "What was the first day of your last menstrual?"

"Um…" I said, drawing a blank.

"Are you still on the Pill?"

"No. I stopped taking it a few months back," I answered, as I pulled my calendar out and tried to count back.

"I see. Besides the migraines, have you been feeling any differently lately?" she asked politely.

"A little tired, but I've been running around a little more than usual so I put it to that," I said, still flipping through the pages for a date.

"Okay. Well why don't we start with a urine sample. Your current condition will dictate what the doctor is able to prescribe for you." "Okay," I easily answered. I seriously doubted that I needed to go through such measures. I had been on the Pill for years and was sure that I was due some sort of reprieve from what she was alluding to. But, I accepted the small cup anyway and then waited for her to come back with the results. Ten minutes passed before she returned with an update.

"We're getting a very weak reading from your urine sample, Ms. Sadiq, so Dr. Amir wants me to draw blood just to be on the safe side."

"What do you mean by weak reading? Everything's okay, right?"

"Yes, I'm sure everything is fine. We just need confirmation that it is before we can properly treat you."

"Okay," I said, as I rolled up my sleeve and watched her poke me.

"Thank ya, ma'am. I shall return," she said before disappearing again.

When she left me alone this time, I started to get a little nervous. What the hell did she mean by a weak reading? I had been taking the Pill for the last five years and only stopped about six months ago. Nothing could have happened that goddamn quick. Shit! I had to calm down. Nothing had been confirmed. It's just with the way my luck had been lately, anything that could happen had happened.

"Knock, knock. Can I come in?" A masculine voice interrupted my thoughts.

"Sure, Dr. Amir."

"And how are you today, Gizelle?"

"Not too good. The migraines have gotten a little worse so I was wondering if you could change my prescription."

"I don't think that will be necessary."

"You don't?"

"No, because I think we've found the source of your headaches."

"You did?" I nervously asked.

"I did. You're pregnant."

"Pregnant? But I was on the Pill."

"Well according to your charts, you stopped taking them a while ago, right?"

"Yeah, but don't they stay in your system for awhile?"

"Sometimes, but the only preventive measure that is one hundred percent is abstinence. I thought you said you were looking forward to having kids the last time you were here."

"I was and I am… I don't know, Dr. Amir. I've got a lot going on right now and I wasn't expecting this."

"I see you don't look like your usual self. Has the morning sickness started already?"

"No, not yet."

"Good. Maybe it'll by pass you. In the interim, here's what I want you to do." I sat there and watched his lips move as he ran down a list of doctors before informing me of what changes my body might experience in the weeks ahead. I was able to nod my head on cue, but I wasn't really listening. My mind had already traveled outside of those four walls and into twelve others that I had recently been in.

"I'm sorry, how far along did you say I was again?" I interjected.

"It's hard to say so early on. I would estimate anywhere from one to six weeks, but your obstetrician should be able to give you a more precise reading. I'll have Amy update your short term forms in case you need a little more time off from work. In the meantime, I want you to get some rest and take it easy. Things can't be that bad."

"Thanks, Dr. Amir. I guess that about covers it, huh?" I said, as I gathered my forms and turned to leave. Guess I was about to get a lot of time off. Talk about being careful what you ask for.

12

"So you keepin' it?" Tracy asked, shortly after I told her that Mekhi and I were expecting. After the doctor's news, it didn't take long for me to realize the only way I would feel an ounce of comfort was to completely exclude any other male from the equation.

"Yeah, I'm keepin' it. Why you ask me that? You know I always wanted a baby."

"Yeah, but right now, Gizelle? I'm sorry but I think you should be weighing your other options first."

"This is my other option. Remember, I vowed I'd never go that other route again. Besides, I think I might need this to settle me down a little."

Lately I had begun to feel like I was in a constant tug of war between choosing what was right and giving in to what was wrong. Dr. Amir's news was slowly bringing things into focus for me. The reality of a child being made in the midst of all that was going on seemed a bit much to be merely coincidental.

"What you're gonna need is a wing, a prayer, and a ring on that finger. Nowadays, even that don't guarantee shit. I don't mean to be harsh, Gizelle, but you gotta think about yourself in all of this. It's different for us than it is for them. Men can pick up and leave whenever they want to but a mother's job is nonstop. I should know, I watch my sisters go through it. You think you're ready for all that?"

"Who says that's gonna be me? Girl, please, you know Mekhi ain't like that. He'll help out," I said, as I looked out the window.

"I'm sure he will if and when he can, but right now you don't even know how the trial is gonna go."

"He'll be all right. He got a top notch lawyer who's hot on the case."

"I hope you're right," Tracy said, under her breath. "How many months are you?"

"Two," I lied, thinking back to the last time Mekhi and I had had sex.

"And where are you gonna stay? I know you ain't going back out to that apartment."

"Girl, hell no. I been moved my stuff from out of there. We're going down to one of his houses."

"Where… down the way?"

"Yeah."

"Oh, *hhheeellll no*! Whose decision was that?" Tracy turned to me and asked.

"Both of ours, why?"

"And you're cool with that?"

"Yeah. Why you say it like that?" I questioned.

" 'Cause that's just askin' for unnecessary drama. People gon' know where y'all live and you know they gon' be all up in your business."

"Girl, please, you know me. I can get real low when I want to and I know how to keep folks out of mine."

"Bump that, *I know them* and it's easy for you to keep ya' shit to yourself when you're far enough away. That shit ain't gone work down there. I'm tellin' you what I know, Gizelle."

"I honestly don't think it'll be that bad, Tracy."

"Shit, you don't know the hood like I do. Them folks thrive off of you and yours and misery loves company. Believe that."

"Hmm, I see," I thought to myself. Right now she seemed like the misery she was talking about. There was something unexplainable in her voice that made her seem more forceful in her argument about our living quarters than her argument about me keeping the baby.

"I thought all his places was rented out anyway. Which one y'all stayin' in?" she finally broke the silence and asked.

"The one with the big yard."

"You sure? Did you ask him, 'cause I thought I saw somebody comin' out of there the other day."

"You probably did. The movers, moving our stuff in."

"I would just ask him, if I were you. Just to make sure," Tracy said, completely ignoring my last comment.

"I don't need to ask him because I just told you I was sure," I said clearly agitated. I had had enough of her bullshit and whatever she thought she wasn't saying, she had already said. I didn't know what the hell she thought she knew, but she was obviously being careful and a little choosy with her words. But, I had had enough of her riddles. I had only stopped by to share my baby news, but was now sorry that I had even done that. I didn't want her reaction or anything she was trying to say to sway my decision away from having the baby. The ringing of my cell broke the silence between us. It couldn't have gone off at a better time.

"Hello…" I answered.

"Holla' at ya' boy."

"*Hello?*"

"Yeah, what you forgot how I sound? It's been that long, huh?" Mekhi joked.

"Yeah, right."

"I need you to come get me."

"All right, I ain't know you was ready. I'll be there in ten minutes."

"Okay."

"Well, let me let you go," Tracy said, as she unlocked the passenger door.

"All right, I'll call you a little later," I lied, before pulling off.

I was all too ready to get away from Tracy and her elusive behavior.

"Daddy's home," Mekhi said as he leaned over and kissed me.

"I missed you, baby," I said, returning his kiss. "Was that Jeremy that just pulled off?" I asked as we drove away from the huge county jail sign. I had spotted him almost immediately after I had arrived, but for some reason he didn't wave. In fact, he almost seemed to glare at me as he drove away.

"Yeah, he ain't know if I had gotten in touch with you and thought I might've needed a ride."

"Oh, okay. How you feelin'?"

"Shit, better now. I couldn't wait to get outta that rotten motherfucker. Them bitches is rotten."

"I know… you poor thing."

"That's okay, I got Canallini gunnin' for their asses… don't you worry your pretty little heart about it."

"I'm not," I said, feeling a whole lot better now that he was right there beside me. "Where you wanna go first? You hungry? Did you eat anything before you left?"

"Naw, I'm good though. I just wanna head over to the new spot and get outta these clothes. Make this right, right here," Mekhi said as we approached an intersection. "Did the boys move all the cars?"

"Yeah, they came and got the keys the other day. Why we goin' this way? I was gonna cut through the park to save some time."

"Naw, it's a straight shot if you keep goin' down this block."

"Huh… to get to the new house?"

"Yeah… oh… I know which way you talkin' 'bout, but we ain't goin' to that house. I had another one done up for us."

"But I thought they moved all of our furniture into the one with the yard."

"Naw."

"Why not?" I asked, feeling myself getting heated.

"Somebody else just moved in there a little while ago."

"Who?"

"Why? You don't know 'em; somebody Jeremy knew. Why, what's up with you? Why so many questions?" Mekhi looked over at me and asked.

"How come you ain't tell me?"

"Cause it wasn't shit to tell. Why you makin' such a big deal out of it?"

" 'Cause I don't understand what the big secret was for."

"Wasn't no secret."

"Swoo…" I loudly exhaled.

"Gizelle, for real? I just got out of jail five minutes ago and you wanna go through this shit right now? I got heavier shit to be thinkin' about, remember? I was gon' tell you, I just got shot before I could, that's all. You making it out to be more than what it is, for real," Mekhi said as I stopped at a red light and turned to gaze out of the window. A tear ran down my cheek and somewhere in the back of my mind, Tracy's words began to echo in my head. I thought about telling him why I was so upset, but decided against it. The truth was I could care less about the house. I was more concerned with the fact that somebody else knew about the whole thing before I did, especially another woman. I wanted so much to be able to suck it all up and let it go, but deep down inside it felt like something else was brewing. And although I didn't know what that something else was, nothing about it seemed good.

Phase II -
Murphy's Law
(Three months later)

13

I was speeding down the highway, jamming off of Cassidy and R. Kelly's new single, "Hotel" when my cell started to vibrate.

"Hey, Ma," I answered.

"Hey, baby, I want you to be still and listen to me for a minute."

"Okay, but I'm in the middle of traffic right now."

"Just listen and be still in your heart, then... you can always be still in your heart Gizelle, even when you're movin' 'round," my grandmother quietly spoke before saying,

"Our Father, who art in heaven,
hallowed be thy name,
thy Kingdom come,
thy will be done,
on earth as it is in heaven,
give us this day our daily bread.
and forgive us our trespasses,

as we forgive those who trespass against us.
And lead us not into temptation,
but deliver us from evil.
For thine is the kingdom,
the power and the glory,
for ever and ever.
Amen."

"I don't know what's going on with you, but it was on my heart to pray over you this mornin'. How're you feelin'?"

"Good, just battling this highway traffic as usual."

"I thought you had to be to work by 8? It's almost ten past right now."

"I do…I overslept, though," I lied as I glanced down at the clock. The truth was if it hadn't been for Mekhi and his goddamn morning quickie, I would've been there by now.

"You know it ain't good to be rushin' 'round baby, 'specially while you carryin', but that ain't why I called you this mornin'. I called you because you been on my mind and my heart somethin' heavy lately, Zella. And I ain't wanna worry you before, but this mornin' I just had to call and check on you and that baby. Is y'all all right?"

"Yeah, except for a little heartburn every now and then, we're doin' okay," I answered as I switched lanes and approached my exit.

"Oh, well all that mean is the baby gon' have a head full of hair like you."

"I know that's what everybody keeps telling me."

"But other than that, has everything been okay?"

"Yeah, as a matter of fact, I had a doctor's appointment the other day. They said I'm a little over five months and that the baby is growing perfectly."

"They still ain't say if it's a boy or girl, huh?"

"No, they couldn't tell because the baby's legs were crossed."

"I guess pretty soon we'll all find out. And what about Mekhi... how's he been doin'?"

"He's good."

"Mmm hhh. Well listen, won't you stop over a little later, that way I can see for myself that everything's okay. Plus, I wanna see just how big you done gotten since the last time I saw you."

"Ma, I'm tellin' you, I'm fine," I tried reiterating. "I've got a few errands to run when I get off."

"You ain't runnin round wit' them old friends of yours is you?"

"What old friends?"

"Them ones you was with that night that car got broken into."

"Naw, Ma, it's been months since I talked to them."

"Well, good. But I still wanna see how big you done gotten."

"All right, well as soon as I come from paying a few bills, I'll stop over."

"Good... hey, Gizelle?"

"Yeah, Ma... I'm still here," I said, as I pulled into the parking lot of my job.

"I know you gotta go, baby, but I gotta say this one last thing before you do. Remember, it ain't good to stress 'bout things you can't do nothin' about. All that'll do is get you one foot into an early grave or a pass into the nut house. When things get too heavy, baby, you turn 'em over and He'll carry 'em for you..."

"Huh? But Ma, I already told you..." I tried interjecting, but it was no use. She kept right on going.

"...Just like that precious bundle growing inside of you. When he gets too heavy, your body will tell you and you'll pop him out. That's the way God planned it, baby. A fool only tries to carry what wasn't his to begin with... tryin' to do God's work. But the Bible says, "To everything there is a season, a time for every purpose under the sun... A time to lose and a time to seek... A time to keep silent and a time to speak. You hear me baby? I said a time to keep silent and a time to speak. You can't let the noise around you drown out His message... you gotta be still and listen. Listen to Him, baby."

"...but Ma, honestly I'm fine, the baby's fine, Mekhi's fine. We're all doing fine," I tried to explain.

"I know you think you are, Zella, but what you learn young, you find useful old. I done learned a long time ago to trust my gut. And right now these old bones is tellin' me otherwise."

"Okay, Ma... well look, I'm at work now and I'm already late, so I'll see you when I get off."

"All right, all right... I'll let you go. I don't like talkin' to you too much on that thing anyway, but you make sure you stop over today, Zella. You hear me?"

"Yeah, Ma. I will," I said before ending the call.

I didn't know how much she thought would happen at work, but if she was praying that I didn't get written up, she was on the right track. I had already been warned twice earlier this week about my lateness.

"Here goes nothing," I said to myself as I attempted to join my coworkers in the huge meeting room. It was Wednesday, which meant that it was time for our mid-week morning huddle. I quickly found a seat in the back row as my supervisor announced, "Team, why don't we all take a ten-minute break and grab some coffee before we get started again. We have a lot of material to cover and I don't want to lose you guys early on in the process."

"Great," I thought to myself as I made a beeline towards the break room.

"…ah, Ms. Sadiq… glad you could join us. Would you come here for a minute, please?" my team leader announced right before I had a chance to make it out of the room.

"Sure. Good morning, Mr. Sudo," I walked up to him and said.

"Good morning, how are you feeling today?"

"Other than a little heartburn, okay I guess."

"I see," he stared at me and said. There was something about his stare that made me feel increasingly uncomfortable. I smoothed my hair and adjusted my clothes just to be sure that there was nothing out of place with me.

"Listen, Suzanne from HR has requested that you come to her office. Do you know where she sits?"

"Yeah, she wants to see me now?"

"Yes, I believe so," he said, with a look of concern.

"Okay," I tried to answer coolly.

Everybody in the office knew Suzanne "The Man" didn't play, and if she wanted to see me it damn sure wasn't about a raise.

Shit. I could've stayed home and went a few more rounds if I knew this shit was coming, I thought to myself as I made my way down to her office. I had already started preparing my defense for my lateness, when the funniest thing happened. A feeling came over me and somewhere in the back of my mind part of my grandmother's morning lecture began to echo in my ears, "...*a time to speak and a time to keep silent... a time to keep silent and a time to speak.*" The message rang so loudly that it completely drowned out any excuses I had brewing in my head.

I opened the door to Suzanne's office, but found no Suzanne. Instead, staring down at me were the same two arrogant motherfuckers from my apartment, that dreadful night of the shooting.

"Hi, remember us?" Detective Shifton asked me.

"Thank you, ma'am, we'll take it from here," Detective Cattlewright said to Suzanne, who now seemed to appear from out of nowhere.

"Ms. Sadiq... You're hereby under arrest. You have the right to remain silent. Anything you say can and will be used against you in a court of law."

I heard what was being said, but couldn't fathom why it was being said. As my hands were brought forth and the handcuffs placed around my wrist, a member of the detective's backup bent down and placed shackles around my ankles.

"Someone get behind her," Detective Cattlewright called out to another member of his crew.

Not knowing what would happen next and too afraid to argue, I silently followed the detectives out of the office, down a path, and into a patrol car that seemed to be waiting just for me.

14

I had been escorted from my workplace and dropped off at an old dilapidated building. In the hours between, my cell, my new Christian Dior bag, and the $4000 I had in it, had been taken from me. And still I had no explanation of exactly what I was being charged with. However, what I did have was a lot of questions, but none of which I felt comfortable enough to ask the huge muscular guard who was guiding me down a narrow, gloomy hall. In my eyes, he was part of the entourage that brought me here. They were all collectively part of a system of corrupt law which far too many times seemed biased, unprincipled, unethical, and just flat out wrong.

"Here you go, Ms. Lady... home, sweet home." The guard snickered as he opened the gate to a dark concrete block. I covered my protruding belly and quietly entered, joining the other prisoners who were already there.

"Damn, Smitty, when you gon' let a bitch use the phone?" a thin, husky- voiced woman asked.

"Who the hell is Smitty?" the guard challenged back.

"Oh, my fault, Brady. But why this shit takin' so long?" she laughed.

"Yeah, and when we gon' eat?" a short, chubby woman whined.

"They got y'all over at County," the guard responded before walking away.

"Shit. Well, I wish they'd come the fuck on then. They keep talkin' 'bout county and the goddamn commissioner," a pale woman said.

"Oh, we done already seen the commissioner, slim. We headin' straight over to County," a seemingly relaxed woman casually interjected.

I stood hushed by their conversation and baffled at the notion of being transported again. I was ready to get the hell out of there. If humiliation and embarrassment had been the detective's goal for me today, it had been accomplished a long time ago.

"When do they let us use the phone?" I broke my silence and asked the relaxed woman. She appeared to be a little more settled than the others.

"You seen the commissioner yet?"

"No."

"You gon' have to see her first to see if she gon' let you out on your own recog', but if you don't see her by a certain time you gon' have to wait till tomorrow."

"Shit, that's what I was afraid of."

I didn't want to stay in there all night. There was only one toilet and one cement block and I was already tired of standing. I exhaled and took off my coat. I wanted to sit and would need to use it as a cushion against the cold concrete.

"Damn, baby girl, you pregnant?" the relaxed woman asked.

"Yeah," I said while trying to comfortably sit on my new pillow.

"Naw, baby girl, you ain't gotta sit on no floor. Sit over there on that block."

"Here, honey, you can sit here if you like," the pale woman said, before getting up.

"No, that's okay."

"Damn, baby girl, how you get yourself in here?"

"I know she ain't no booster 'cause I know 'em all and I ain't never seen her," the chubby woman said.

I turned back towards the relaxed woman before responding, "I don't know. My boyfriend was robbed… then shot outside of my house and when I called for help the police came…"

"…into your place and found all that shit… yeah… I remember. I read all about it in the paper. Damn, baby, that was you, huh?" she interrupted, shaking her head. She continued, "Baby girl, don't you know you don't let no nigga' keep that shit where you sleep?"

I heard what she said, but had never had it put to me that way before. For a split second, I felt like a child being scorned and right before I could respond, Brady reappeared and gestured for me to come with him.

"You're going into see the commissioner," he said, as he led me into a small office room.

Inside of the room sat a middle-aged, newly blonde-haired woman buried behind stacks of paper. I sat in a chair directly opposite of her and silently waited until she finished reading over what I assumed to be my charge papers.

"Bail is set at $150,000," she finally said.

"Dag, that's how you feelin'," Brady commented.

"How I'm feelin'? Have you seen this sheet?"

"No, not yet."

"Here, let me do you the honors," she said, while handing the papers over to him.

"Wow, that ain't pretty."

"My sentiments exactly," she said, shortly before dismissing me.

"Do I get my phone call now?" I asked Brady, as I followed him back down the long, dark hall.

"Yeah, once they transport y'all over to the county jail. Here you go," he said, as he opened the cell back up.

"Hey, you back. What they say?" the chubby woman asked.

I only glanced at her before taking my same Indian-style seat on the floor.

"Baby girl, did they let you use the phone?" the relaxed woman asked.

"No, not yet."

"Don't worry. I'll call your folks for you when we get over to County. They gon' take me back first 'cause I'm comin' back in from work release."

"Oh, okay... thank you... what happens once we get over there?"

"They'll probably get you processed and take you up on Medical. Medical's cool."

"What's Medical?"

"One of the dorms over there."

"Oh."

"You'll be all right. Just keep ya shit to yourself."

"How long you been in here?" I decided to ask.

"Eight months this time, but I'm on my way out and once I leave, I ain't never comin' back," she stated right before Brady re-emerged to escort us to our transportation.

As we started our commute, I sat there and thought about my day. There I sat, sandwiched between two females that I would probably never see again in life. I was going to a place that I had never been to before in life, wondering how I got there and wishing that I wasn't. I felt like I was being punished for something I hadn't done.

We made one stop to pick up more prisoners before we were finally all unloaded and crammed into a holding cell referred to as the "bullpen", at the women's county jail.

"Hey, thanks again, I really appreciate it," I said to my relaxed friend after I gave her Mekhi's number.

"Don't worry about it. I'll call him as soon as I get up to my dorm. Hey… what's your name again?"

"Gizelle," I answered, as they opened the cell bars to let her out. As she took off up a flight of stairs she looked back once more and shouted, "Hey, Gizelle, don't worry. I got you covered, baby girl."

"Thank you… ahh… ummm… what's *your* name? You didn't tell me your name," I yelled back.

"Angel, they call me Angel," she said, disappearing up the stairs.

Angel… I thought to myself, *…how fitting.*

Another hour would pass before it would be my turn to fade away up those same stairs, but when I did, I immediately went to work on my exit strategy.

15

"*Tomorrow*? I don't want to stay in this depressing-ass place overnight. Do you know what they made me do? They made me take off my clothes and then squat and cough, Mekhi... squat and cough!" I angrily charged back.

"Huh? They know you pregnant right?"

"I was butterball-ass naked. How could they not know?!"

"Gizelle, listen baby, I don't want you in there just as much as you don't wanna be in there, and you know that. But we on their playin' field right now, baby, and my hands are tied only because they haven't put you all the way in the system yet."

"And what happens if I still ain't all the way in there by tomorrow?"

"Then your lawyer knows he needs to go and meet with the judge."

"So you're saying I gotta stay in here until he comes from seeing him?"

"No, that's not what I said. Listen, just let me take care of things on my end and I promise we'll have this shit squared away first thing tomorrow morning," Mekhi tried his best to reassure me.

"Ssswwwoooo," I slowly exhaled.

"I know it's tough, baby, but please try not to stress about it, at least for the baby's sake. All right?"

"I hear you, Mekhi, but that's just it, nothing about this seems all right. *Especially* for the baby's sake."

"That's because this shit is wrong on multiple levels, but we'll talk more about it once you get home, okay?"

"Okay. Well, I guess I should go find a bunk. Plus, I just overheard somebody say they're about to serve us lunch. I'll try to call you back a little later," I said right before ending the call. I was in a rush to get off the phone with him. I didn't want to lash out at him anymore than I already had. It wasn't his fault that these assholes were being jerks. I was just irritated with the whole situation. I tucked my bed sheets under one arm and ventured out to find my sleeping quarters for the night.

All in all, there were about ten cells caged off from the rest of the jail's population and even though the cage was locked, the cells within it remained open.

Outside of each cell and lined up against the caged bars, were extra cots for more prisoners. I guess the criminal population had quickly outgrown what the jail's capacity could hold, although for the life of me I couldn't understand why. Nothing about this place was appealing. The space was cramped and the mysterious and murky cells left me wondering what secrets they held. In fact, with the exception of being isolated from the other inmates, this so called "medical dorm" was no different from any other jail I had ever seen on television. I couldn't imagine ever getting use to it, even though some of the images around me gave clear indications that it was indeed possible.

Some of the prisoners had towels and sheets hung like decorative curtains and makeshift picture frames taped to the cold concrete walls. Others had magazine racks and crafty baskets filled with goodies. A few of them even had their own versions of doormats outside the entrances of their cells.

"It couldn't be me," I thought to myself. But in reality, right now, it was me. It was me and my unborn child sitting there on an uncomfortable cot in the middle of what seemed like a whirlwind circle called my life and for what? Sure, I had a few vices, but I wasn't a bad person and I definitely wasn't a criminal, so why was I there? Had the detectives taken shit that personal or had I really done something wrong to deserve this? This should've been a joyous time for me, the happiest nine months of my life; yet things continued to go from bad to worse, instead of from better to best. And I just couldn't understand why. Why was so much happening and why was it happening to *me*?

"Hey, I thought you'd be gone by now." The familiar face interrupted my thoughts. The booster lady and some of the others who had traveled there with me were walking my way.

"Me, too," I said under my breath.

"How much longer you got?"

"I should be gone by tomorrow."

"Naw, I meant before the baby comes."

"Oh... around four months," I answered.

"You havin' a boy ain't you?" the thin, husky-voiced woman asked.

"I don't know, my doctors couldn't tell."

"Don't need no doctor to see that. You glowin' and all, baby. A baby girl take all that shit from you. Believe me I know, I got five of them sassy motherfuckers."

"You got five girls?" I asked.

"Yup, and I ain't look nothin' like you when I was carryin' them, either. Did I, little Mama?" she asked and turned towards the booster lady for confirmation.

"Hell naw and ya ass was evil as shit, too."

"Yeah, she was," another woman chimed in.

"Y'all been knowing each other for a while?" I decided to ask.

"Naw, but I had my last one while I was in here."

"Oh, okay," I answered, but in the back of my mind I wondered *how much trouble did you have to be in to have a child while incarcerated?*

"It's much better up here, ain't it girl? We got ice, a TV, and everything. Just don't use the Lisa soap; yo' shit, won't ever be the same if you do," the booster woman proudly said, interrupting my thoughts again.

"The what?" I asked.

"*The Lisa soap,*" she answered, while pointing to some of the signs posted by the inmates around the dorm. "That's the soap they give out for free, but that shit so potent, I swear they ought'a be able to kill cancer wit' it. If you need some soap, just let me know. Just don't use that shit," she said, and laughed.

I politely smiled, but hardly found any of what she was saying funny. I had heard enough and was more than ready to go. Boy, oh boy, tomorrow couldn't come fast enough.

Lunch was horrible. When the call for dinner came, I quickly fell in line behind the others, hoping I'd be able to recognize what was being served. From what I could tell, some type of red dish was being handed out, but I still couldn't quite make out what it was. The inmate serving it looked awfully familiar, though. I caught a glimpse of her while watching the others dodge in and out of line. From where I stood, she appeared to be flawless: smooth even-toned skin, a perfect natural arch in her brow, and a body to die for. How had such a pretty girl wound up in such an ugly place, and why was she sportin' a one blade? Even with no hair she was beautiful.

Although I didn't want to be recognized in here, it was killing me to find out who she was. So when my turn came in line, I stood in front of her and cleared my throat but all she did was pass a tray and wait for me to move. I just didn't get it. Why did she seem so familiar? As I joined the other inmates down at the eating table, I looked back once more and caught her smirking at me and suddenly it hit me.

Oh shit, I thought to myself. *It just couldn't be!* I needed confirmation and I knew exactly who would give it to me, but I would need to wait to avoid seeming so obvious. Almost an hour went by before I found the thin, husky-voiced woman sitting alone on her bunk.

"Hey, what's up wit' ya young'un? You seem kind of dazed. Everything a'ight?"

"Yeah, just ready to get the hell out of here."

"I here that. Ain't we all."

"Yeah, I guess so… who was that girl that delivered our food tonight?"

"Which one?"

"The one with the close-cut."

"Who, the Spanish-lookin' one?"

"Yeah… her."

"Oh, that's Ya, but don't nobody really talk to her. Why? You know her?"

"No, I don't think so, but she kinda look like somebody I use to know. But the girl I'm thinkin' about had a lot of hair."

"Oh yeah, she did…when she first got here, but when everybody started goin' after her she cut it real low. Real pretty girl, just ain't my cup of tea and I would stay away from her if I were you. She got trouble written all over her. I know her type and they sneaky, plus they say she pregnant."

"Yeah, now you tell me," I said under my breath.

"What you say young'un?"

"Oh nothing, just listening."

"Yeah… I did hear something about her leaving, though… I think they dismissed her charges… 'least I think that's what I heard somebody say."

"Oh," I said, feeling a little relieved.

"Yeah, she got fed time coming. Conspiracy or drug trafficking or somethin' like that... Ya... Ya... Yasmine...that's her name."

"Hey, Mother Earth," a distant voice interrupted from the opposite side of the cage. "Y'all got a Mother Earth up here?" the inmate asked.

"They callin' you young'un'," the thin, husky-voiced woman said to me.

"Huh?" I questioned.

"Mother Earth means carryin'...and you the only one up here who pregnant."

"Oh... yeah," I nervously answered, while moving in the direction the distant voice was coming from.

"Here, somebody told me to give you this."

"Me?"

"Yeah, I guess. She said look out for the pretty pregnant one with the long hair, so here you go," she said, before passing me a bag full of several different types of snacks and a note which read, "Make sure you feed that baby."

"Wait, who sent this... hey, who gave these to you?" I yelled out to the note passer, but it was too late. She was already gone.

Phase III -

Nine Months Later

Same cast - different script

16

"Eight and 1/2 pounds, are you serious? I know your ass was in there carryin' on like crazy," Mackenzie, my former coworker, said before bursting into laughter.

"You know I was. You know I ain't one for pain, and by the time I was done, everybody on that damn hospital floor knew it, too," I said, giggling myself.

"I still can't believe you had a baby. What's his name again?"

"Journey... Journey-Mekhi. Wait until you see him, girl. He's a mini-me. He's got a head full of dark curly hair and the most adorable brown eyes you've ever seen in your life. I just can't stop kissing him."

"Awww, he sounds so cute. I can't wait to see him."

"Well, you better hurry up. You know he's almost four months now."

"Damn, already? That was quick. The last time I saw you, you were still wobbling around that damn office."

"I know and I was close to five months then. Come to think of it, the last time I saw you, they were escorting me out of that goddamn office."

"Wow, I think you're right, Gizelle. I didn't realize it had been so long. I thought you were gonna try and come back."

"I thought I was too, but the more time went by, I started thinkin' that maybe they had already fired me and was just waitin' on me to come back so that they could do it in person."

"What made you think somethin' like that?"

" 'Cause none of them ever tried to get in touch with me… somethin' about the whole thing just ain't seem right."

"Yeah, but can they just up and fire you?"

"Girl, who you askin'? Don't get me to lyin'. I don't know if they can or if they can't, but I damn sure knew that I wasn't stickin' around to find out."

"I feel you."

"Besides, it's been too long to try and come back now. Plus, with the baby and everything else I got going on, I ain't hardly thinkin' about that place."

"I know you're not. How did everything end up working out with you anyway?" Mackenzie asked, hinting around to my charges. I knew it was coming sooner or later, but I had long before made a personal vow not to discuss *anything,* about my brief jail stay with *anybody.* And because that included Mekhi, it included Mackenzie, too. Besides, nothing had ever come of it, so why start rehashing things now? I planned on keeping the whole thing buried in the back of my head.

"Mekhi is taking all the charges," I finally said.

"Oh. Was it a lot?"

"Yeah, I'd say they were hefty."

"For real?"

"Yeah, he's facing up to twenty."

"Twenty years?!" Mackenzie shockingly asked.

"Yeah, but I don't wanna discuss it right now. It's way too depressing. What's been going on with you?" I asked, quickly switching the subject.

"Well, I was gonna wait to tell you this in person, but I guess now is as good of a time as any," Mackenzie said before pausing. "Girl, I got married."

"What? You lyin', Mack, for real? I don't believe you," I said and laughed.

"Girl, I ain't lyin'."

"For real, to who?"

"No…wait there's more…we're also expecting our first child."

"Hold up, now I know you're lyin'," I said, laughing even harder.

"No, I'm serious, Gizelle." she said, smiling through the phone. "You remember that guy I used to always go out to lunch with?"

"Yeah."

"Well, long story, short… he asked and I said yes. Then about three months ago, we went down to the courthouse and low and behold… here I is," she chuckled before continuing, "*I's married now.*"

"Wow, Mack… I mean, I knew you two were dating, but I would've never guessed things had gotten so serious. Why you ain't call and tell me?"

"Girl, I wanted to call you so bad, but I knew you had a lot going on, so I just kept it quiet until now."

"Oh my goodness, I just can't believe it. Well, how does it feel?" I asked, still in a state of disbelief.

"Absolutely wonderful. He totally adores me, Gizelle, and he spoils me even more. He won't let me do anything for myself and I love it, too. I am so in love with this man, girl. Do you hear me? I swear, now I know how you've been feelin' about Mekhi for all these years."

"Well, I guess congratulations are in order. I'm really happy for you, Mack," I lied. "I guess me and Journey are the ones who should be paying you a visit."

"Girl, please, you sound just like my husband and I'm gonna tell you just like I tell him, I can still get around. I'm a little over one month, not ten. Besides, I really could use the outing and the fresh air will do some good. Speaking of babies, where is that little angel of yours anyway? It's been mighty quiet over there. Is he out with that proud daddy of his?"

"No, actually he's in the house with my grandmother. You know how those great-grandparents can be, stealin' babies every chance they get," I laughed.

"Awww, that sounds really sweet."

"But listen, you must have talked his proud daddy up 'cause that's him calling on the other line now. I'll call you back a little later after I finish running my errands."

"Okay, well tell Mekhi I said hi, and kiss the baby for me."

"Okay, I will."

There was no one on my other line. I had purposely lied to get off the phone with her. I just couldn't believe she had run off and gotten married and was now expecting, too? That was my fairytale ending not hers, so why had she been so privileged? I was the one who had put in the time and I was the one who had just had a baby, so quite naturally I was the one who should've been shouting, *"I's married now,"* not her.

And it had taken her all of thirty seconds to remind me.

How could I truly be happy for Mackenzie when I had my own happiness at stake? It seemed like ever since Journey had been born and Mekhi's mandatory sentencing guidelines had been handed down, things had gone back to the way they used to be. Mekhi had regressed and he was back to his old late night habits again. More and more, I felt the strain of being forced into a role of single parenting and the loneliness that came with it seemed unbearable. Sure, I had the baby, but I was a woman way before I became a mother, and the woman in me missed the feelings of adoration and admiration and anything else that came with being in a loving relationship. What was becoming of me and Mekhi? We had a brand new baby, for goodness sake. So why was it that Journey seemed more like mine instead of ours, and how had things gotten so bad so fast when they had been so good for so long? Getting back to true happiness felt like an unending maze and made me question if I ever really knew it in the first place.

"Sswwhhoo," I sighed, as I tried to re-focus. "Get it together, Gizelle," I said to myself as I pulled into the mall's parking garage. I hopped out of my truck and ran right into two old familiar faces.

"Oh my goodness, Kiera Mitchell and Trina Briggs. What wind blew you two in?" I said, as I turned to embrace my childhood friends.

"We should be askin' your crazy butt the same thing," Trina jokingly said.

"Oh my God, Gizelle, look at you. You're a grown ass woman now," Kiera smiled and commented.

"I know, right? That's usually what happens to little girls over time," I said and laughed.

"Girl, you know what I mean. It's been a month of Sundays since I last saw you. How have you been?"

"Good. What about y'all?"

"We're good. Trina told me that you just had a baby."

"I did. It's been almost four months now, though."

"Wow. I didn't even know that you were pregnant."

"What? I thought everybody from 'round the way knew."

"Everybody 'cept for me. You know I'm always the last one to ever find out about anything. You got any pictures on you?"

"I think so, hold up," I said, as I searched my bag for recent photos.

"I hope you got some extras, 'cause I want one. I saw her and Mekhi out the other day and she is so cute."

"Really? I said, half-listening, as I continued to rummage through my bag. "Mekhi ain't even tell me that he saw you," I said, as I handed them both a picture.

"Girl, I don't think he saw… oh," Trina paused before saying, "I thought you had a little girl."

"Nope, a big-headed little boy," I joked. "What made you think I had a girl?"

"I just thought I saw Mekhi carrying a baby in all pink. Maybe it was somebody else then," Trina tried to explain, as she puzzlingly gazed at the picture. She wasn't slick and I could tell that her childish instigating ways had followed her well into adulthood. Kiera must have picked up on it too, because she tried to break the tension by saying, "Girl you know Trina can't hardly see. You remember how she couldn't never find us when we use to play, Hide and Go-Seek."

"Shut up, Kiera. Gizelle, he is really handsome."

"Thank you."

"What's his name?"

"Journey-Mekhi."

"Aww, that's so cute. I bet you're spoiling him like crazy."

"You know I am. I can't help it. He's our real-life baby doll."

"Where is he now?" Kiera asked.

"With my grandmother. I only came out to grab some diapers and wound up around here at the mall."

"Well look, don't let us hold you up. We know how important time can be for a new mom," Kiera said.

"Yes, Lord," Trina added, as we hugged once more and said our goodbyes.

I pretended to look for something inside of my glove box as I watched them both disappear inside of the mall. Once they were no longer in sight, I started the truck and headed back towards my grandmother's house. Suddenly, I didn't feel much like shopping anymore.

It had taken me all of twenty minutes to scoop up Journey and make my way back in the house. Once I did, as usual, I was the only adult there. Tonight it didn't matter though, because I planned on being by the door, armed with a mouthful once Mekhi finally came strolling through it. So far, I had held off calling him for fear that I might say too much over the phone and have him deliberately trying to avoid me. The nerve of him, *and Trina too,* for that matter. I should've known better than to stop and talk to her instigating ass. Not only had she just given me a headache, but she had also given me another issue to deal with at home.

"…thought you had a girl," she said. "…maybe it was somebody else," she teased. She knew it was him and deep down inside, I knew it too. The only thing I didn't know was: a) why he would be out playin' Daddy when he had a child of his own waiting at home; b) what other roles he had been out playing; and c) what he could possibly be thinking. I had abandoned all of my bad habits and mischievous ways and he was out creating new ones. Well, his ass better have a good explanation for this one, because my patience was wearing thin. All of the rumors coupled with his nonchalant attitude were starting to add up to the demise of our enchanted fable. I was beginning to question if the path I had chosen had been the right one.

"Get it together, Gizelle. You will get through this just like you got through all the other bullshit," I tried to reassure myself. But the truth was, my tolerance for Mekhi's drama had become increasingly low ever since the baby was born. Right now I needed to be soothed and reminded of what being a woman felt like. I had long since healed from the pain of labor and delivery, but my sex life had yet to pick up where my fantasies had left off. If Mekhi's gestures of affection were a little more consistent, maybe I wouldn't be so tense right now. They had become so rare that my body continuously yearned for the sensual caress of another. Someone or some two, who would be delighted by my wild sexual nature, as I willingly and enthusiastically took pleasure in theirs.

I nestled Journey inside of his bassinette and slipped into a tub full of relaxing warm water. "Hmmm." I slowly exhaled and laid my head back as I let the serenity of the moment massage my troubled mind. I was beginning to learn that there was something calming about being in a moment of stillness. More times than others, it brought comfort and gave me an opportunity to reflect. "Mmmm." I sighed again just as the phone began to ring loudly in the background.

"Shit!" I said, as I leaped from the tub in an attempt to catch it before it woke Journey.

"Hello… Hello?" I panted out.

"Hello, you have a text to landline message…" the computerized voice instructed before the message began to play.

"…Hey, baby, haven't heard from you and been worried sick. I'm sorry about the other day, but I promise to make it up to you. I love you and I hope you have a good day in court tomorrow." (Click)

I rushed over to the ID box to pull up the caller's information, but the batteries were weak and the number was too faint to read. "….bbbrrriiinnnggg… bbbrrriiinnnggg." The phone rang again.

"Hello… Hello," I quickly answered, but the line went dead.

This time, I immediately dialed *69, but the automated voice informed me that the caller's information was unavailable. There I stood, dripping wet, cradling the phone and replaying the message in my head. Who in the hell was calling my house, apologizing and confessing her love to my man, before wishing him well for a court date that I knew nothing about?

"Shit," I said out loud, as I quickly dialed Mekhi's cell. And when he didn't answer, I tried dialing again, and then again, and then again. But, still there was no answer.

I'm so tired of this shit. When will it ever end? I asked myself while pacing from one room to the next. My mind was racing in a million different directions, as I slowed down to take in all the costly images surrounding me. A $3000 mahogany bassinette, a $9500 convertible, handmade crib, a $1700 Amish-style carrier, two brand new Yves Saint Laurent bags, two brand new pairs of Hermes…

What are you doing, Gizelle? Just let it go. You've got everything a new mother or any woman could want right here. Here is where your security lies. Why can't you just leave well enough alone? You know when you go looking for trouble you find it, the voice inside of my head cautioned.

"...but I'm not looking for trouble. I'm looking for answers," I silently answered back. *So what then? You're just gonna take that baby outside at this time of night?* I just sat there for a moment and took it all in. I wanted so badly to give in to my inner voice, but tonight there was something inside of me that just wouldn't let things rest. I dialed Mekhi's cell once more, and when he didn't answer that time, I packed a small bag for Journey and myself before leaving out of the house. I needed some fresh air and I planned on taking the scenic route in order to get it. I would show his ass who had the upper hand once and for all.

17

It was a cool September night and once I was actually outside of the house, part of me felt kind of foolish for having Journey out there so late. But I was on a mission and right now my conflicted mind couldn't see past the affairs of my foolish heart. I sat in my room and tried to play things down, but it was no use—that call had given me the much needed ammunition to demand answers from Mekhi's cheating ass. And if he was too preoccupied to give them to me over the phone, then he would definitely be giving them to me face-to-face. I couldn't believe him. I spent night after night at home alone, tossing and turning, waiting and hoping for him to come in and comfort me; only to find myself eventually drifting off as night turned into day. If I refused to acknowledge the fact that my adoring prince was no more, I had no choice but to do so now. Mekhi had unquestionably changed. And so tonight, midnight found me outside with my newborn, on a hunt to catch my so called prince in all of his wrong-doings. The funny thing was, I had a gut feeling of exactly where to begin my search: the house we should've been living in.

I never really bought his reason as to why we couldn't stay there, but at the time I had no choice but to accept it. And now, as I approached the block, to say that I was shocked by the number of big ticket cars that stuck out would be an understatement. Other than Mekhi's 760 Li, there was a brand new CL AMG, a Bentley GT Coupe, a Range Rover HSE that looked similar to mine, and a few other high-priced noticeables. It didn't take long for me to gather that there was some type of party going on inside of the home, but what I couldn't figure out was why in the world Mekhi was there. According to him, his lawyer had cautioned for us both to stay away from the house because of something involving his case. So why then, was he here partying and more importantly, why wasn't I invited? Something about the whole picture didn't look right.

I pulled up behind his car and sat there long enough to witness a few girls go in and a few fellas come out, some of whom even seemed to be bearing gifts. Damn it, Mekhi! What was the big goddamn secret? He told me about any other festivities, so what was so different about this one? And if this was some type of going away party, shouldn't I have been included? I circled the block while thinking of a way to approach the whole situation. I could simply walk in as if I was supposed to be there. Hell, I was still his woman so no one would dare say anything to me out of the way. Then again, I had Journey with me and I didn't want to look crazy for having him dangling from my hip at this time of night. Maybe if I dropped him off with my grandmother and then came back, but what if the party ended or Mekhi left before I returned?

"Shit! Gizelle, think... think... think! There's gotta be a way to catch him while still keeping my image intact." I said to myself as I stopped at a traffic light. I was so engulfed with my thoughts that for a moment I totally forgot about Journey being in the backseat. It was his precious little whine that snapped me back into reality.

"What are you doing Gizelle?" I thought to myself as I peeked back at him. From the way his car seat was positioned, all I could see was the top of his tiny head.

"Think about all that you're about to do... what sense does it make? Especially when you know he'll probably give you some excuse that you'll most likely believe, a few big gifts, which will most likely position

things back to normal again... at least until the next fuck up," my inner voice calmly spoke to me.

"And what good is that gonna do?" I questioned myself.

"What good is acting out gonna do? You shouldn't be out here and neither should that baby. Why don't you just go back into the house? He'll be in sooner or later."

"...but what if he doesn't?"

"He will and you know he will. Think about the last time something like this happened."

"But, this never happened before at least not like this... not after Journey arrived."

"Exactly, things would be different if it was just you, but it's not and that baby doesn't deserve to be out here this time of night in the middle of grown folks' business."

"Agh! Fuck!" I said, while banging the steering wheel. I didn't know if I was coming or going. Of all the times Mekhi would pick to show his ass it would be now, after the baby was born. Well, I had something for his ass. Two could play at this game. I made a U-turn and drove back past the *other house* again, only this time I was too caught up in my own emotions to notice the half-deflated *"It's a girl"* balloon tied to the outside stair rail.

I would show up for court tomorrow to get all the answers that his ass was too busy to give me tonight. I would play his little game and go back in the house, but not before paying a visit to an old faithful friend.

"Get in here... and take off them clothes."

It was just the invitation I needed to be led from out of the cool night air and into the warm, enticing darkness. I had spent almost an hour outside pondering whether or not what I was about to do was right. It had been a while since our last encounter and I knew being here was a little risky, but tonight I didn't care. And now, as I relaxed my body and tried to let go of my anxieties, I gradually surrendered to the irresistible feeling. We were almost an hour into our full-blown freak session and I stood drunk with passion, sandwiched against a wall, feeling captive in erotic heaven. To say that I was in pure ecstasy would be putting it mildly; it was sheer and utter bliss. The throbbing feeling behind me only accentuated what was going on in front of me and for the life of me I couldn't figure out which one was more pleasing. I slowly opened my legs, giving way to the unknown wonders of what seemed to be a magic tongue and shivered as my lips were descriptively traced from the outside-in.

"Mmmm… agh… sss… just like that… mmm… don't stop," I pleaded to the one between my legs.

"…you like that, Mommy?"

"Yes… wait… uh… right there…do it, baby." I threw my head back and moaned.

"Mmm… do it bitch," the one behind me whispered in my ear as we continued our slow grind. Back and forth, forth then back, we compulsively rocked before eventually making our way over to the couch.

"Come here… you ready for this dick?" she seductively whispered, while pulling me her way. I eagerly watched as she slowly massaged all eight inches of what was attached to her.

"Agh… mmm!" I squealed, as she turned me around, grabbed my hips, and pulled me down on top of her.

"You gon' take all of it?" she asked, as she slid into the core of my wetness.

"Mmmm… yes, baby, yes!"

The one who had been in between my legs closely followed behind before climbing on top of me and starting her own enthused grind.

"Agh, Gizelle… no!"

"You like that… tell me it's good!" I demanded, as I slid my fingers inside of her.

"Oh God, yes! It's good… it's so good." she screamed out. I repositioned one of her legs inside of mine and guided her hips; perfectly aligning her clit against mine. I traced one of her nipples with my tongue before asking, "You sure?"

"Mmm... yes... it's so good. Mmmm... wait."

"Wait, shit... give me this pussy, bitch."

"No... Agh, yes."

"Mmm... agh!" I screamed out, as the one behind me lunged deeper inside.

"Tell me it's good!"

"It's good!"

"Mmm... say it again, bitch!"

"Mmm... it's good... it's so fucking good!" I hollered out, as she pulled me back closer.

The methodic rhythm of her clit against mine coupled with the consistent vibration within, had me drunk with passion and drenched heavily with lust. The two of them combined were reaching each and every spot imaginable. Never had it been this good.

"Is this my pussy?"

"Yes."

"...say it again, bitch!" she demanded as she smacked my ass.

"Agh... it's yours, baby. It's yours... mmm... it's so fucking good!"

"You sure?"

"Yes, baby, yes."

"You gon' suck it?"

"Mmm... yes, Mommy."

"You promise?"

"Agh... oh God, yes!"

"Take it out and put it in your mouth," she commanded as she begun to fuck me even harder.

"Agh... wait... no, I can't!"

"I said take it out, bitch!"

"No, baby wait... agh, it's so good!" I screamed out, while trying to keep up with her.

"Mmm... take it out and lick that pussy juice off it," she said again, as she pulled the two of us back and started a tongue war with us.

"You gon' lick it?"

"Yes... baby... yes."

"Lay back and show me," she said, as she pulled it out.

"No, lay back and *show me*," he said, as he got up from where he had been sitting and walked over to the three of us. *"It's my turn now!"*

18

I had tried to make things right between Mekhi and me, but he was just too caught up in his own shit to give a damn. And now, just like countless times before, his selfishness and lack of attention had landed me smack dab in the middle of a *very* compromising situation. Never in a million years would I have guessed that things would've gotten as freaky as they had last night, but things took off so fast that it was hard not to give in to the overwhelming sensation of it all. One minute, I was playfully stripping down and the next, I was sitting on somebody's face while somebody else was sitting on mine. A few hours and even more orgasms later, I was giddy and child-like, trying to sneak back into my grandmother's house. I had left Journey with her, claiming to have something important to take care of. Now that morning had arrived, guilt was beginning to seep in and regret was starting to get the best of me. I had done many things before, but a lot of what had taken place last night had been a first for me. The question that kept repeating itself in my head was, "How would I ever live this one down?"

It was now 7 a.m. and Journey was beginning to wiggle beside me. I peeked to see if he was awake and found him wide-eyed, staring back at me.

"Well, Good morning to you too, pumpkin. And how did *you* sleep?" I asked, in my playful baby's tone before picking him up and kissing his soft cheeks. In spite of everything that was going on, my little bundle of joy always seemed so peaceful and calm, as if he didn't have a care in the world. Even for a baby, it seemed oddly unusual. I secretly wished I could steal that part away from him and keep it for myself. That way I could drown out the constant noise surrounding me and focus all of my attention on him.

"Oh, what's the matter?" I said, as he started to cry.

"All right, all right, I know you're hungry," I said, as I leaned over and picked up a bottle. Since I still wasn't sure what time the court proceedings would start, I got up out of bed and cleaned and dressed Journey before I cleaned and dressed myself. I didn't know all that would go on in court, but I was determined to get answers to all of the questions I had from last night. I combed my long, dark tresses down into my trademark feathered wrap and checked my-self out in the huge floor length mirror. My pinstripe Gucci suit had been tailored to delicately fit each one of my curves, my face had been painted on with the best of M.A.C.'s natural hues, and my 4-inch Gucci pumps enhanced the overall effect while adding high fashion to my persona. A wide clutch plus a few dia-monds strategically placed, and my ensemble was complete. My look was more than smooth, it was high-end fashion and perfection at its best. I only hoped that all I was about to walk into would go as smoothly as my appearance.

"Follow Mommy's lead, pumpkin," I whispered in my little baby's ear. Even though I hadn't planned on taking Journey with me, I had him dressed as if he were going as well.

"Good morning, Ma," I said, as I walked into my grandmother's kitchen.

"Good mornin' and mornin' to you too, hand-some," she said, as she reached out for Journey. "I thought you had a court hearing this mornin'?"

"I do," I said, as I opened the fridge and started transferring Journey's bottles over to his baby bag.

"You ain't plannin' on takin' this baby wit' you is you?"

"Yeah, I was."

"Now, Gizelle, you know a court ain't no place for no child."

"I thought you had some errands to run."

"Well if I did, I'd just take this little handsome man wit' me."

"Oh, okay. Thanks, Ma," I said, as I began to put the bottles back into the fridge.

"Just look at him, he just as precious as he wanna be… got an old soul, too. He ain't nothin' but a blessing Gizelle, straight from above," she said, as she adjusted Journey in her arms.

"Thanks, Ma," I said, keeping my answers short and sweet. I was planning on making a beeline straight towards the front door. "Okay Ma, well I'll be back as soon as the hearing is over," I said, as I bent down to kiss Journey on his head.

"Oh, Gizelle?"

"Yeah?" I called out from the hallway. *Keep goin' keep goin' keep goin',* I coached myself.

"Can you come back in here for a second, please?"

Shit, I knew it! I was in no fucking mood for a church session this morning.

"Yeah, Ma," I politely answered from the kitchen doorway.

"What's been going on here with you lately?" she asked, as she calmly rocked the baby.

"What do you mean?"

"I thought things had calmed down for you a bit."

"*They have*," I said, while glancing up at the clock. I was trying my best to hide my frustration, but I was clearly annoyed.

"Well, I can't tell. You drivin' round wit' this baby all hours of the night doin' only God knows what wit' God knows who."

"I wasn't driving around with him last night. I told you I came straight over here after I met up with Mekhi," I stretched the truth.

"And what time was that Gizelle?"

"I don't know. As soon as I left him we…"

"Oh, hush now and let me stop you for you fall into the hole you keep tryin' to dig for somebody else. Who you think you foolin'?"

"I'm not fooling nobody."

"Now that's the first decent thing I don' heard you say this mornin'. You keep goin' on and on wit' this story, lyin' about Mekhi and…"

"What story? I ain't lyin' about…"

"Gizelle, hush! Now you know you ain't left that boy last night as sure as I'm standin' here in front of you this mornin'. Mekhi been over *here* lookin' for *you* last night. Now you listen to me and you listen good 'cause He done gave you enough warnings and I ain't sure how many more you got 'fore things really start to fallin' apart on you."

"Who done gave me enough warnings?"

"Obviously, not the one you was wit' last night!" she snapped back.

"Sswwoo…" I exhaled loudly.

"A woman should have better values and more respect for herself and for God's sake, more discretion. Now I know He's working on you, that much I can see for myself, but you gotta work wit' Him too, child and all this foolishness you doin' out here in the street ain't right. You just remember you reap what you sow."

"But why you ain't sayin nothin' about what he out there doin'? He left me and Journey and you in here defendin' him and…"

"Defendin' who?"

"Mekhi," I said, as the tears began to fall uncontrollably.

"Are you listenin' to me or are you simply entertainin' what's in that head of yours? Ain't nobody defendin' him. This ain't no more about him than it is the stranger out there on the street. Who cares that he out there …what you gonna do, make him stay in? Gizelle, I ain't sayin' you wrong for feelin' the way you do, but you ain't right for actin' out in the way that you is, either. Ain't nobody forcin' you to stay in a place that you feel ain't worthy of your being. If it's too much or… if it ain't what you signed on to do… guess what …you can always leave! But the one thing you can't do is force your lessons onto somebody else. What God has for you is *for you,* honey, no matter what it is. Now you can do one of two things: You can start worryin' about your own shit or you can continue to sniff his," she said, as she handed me a tissue to blow my nose.

"Look at me, baby. As much as you want it to be, this ain't about him. You gotta understand that," she said and paused. "As you go through life you'll learn that sometimes… things ain't always meant to last forever. Sometimes people grow apart and when that time come you gotta be careful what choices you make 'cause the one thing you can't get back is time. You get what I'm sayin'?"

"Yeah," I said between tears.

"Everybody ain't always meant to stay in the front row of your life baby, sometimes you gotta move 'em up to the balcony. 'Cause if you handin' out free tickets and ain't getting nothin' back in return, then who's the fool? And I'ma tell you something else… sometimes naïve young girls turn into used and bitter old women. Don't you let that be you," she said, as she tilted my head upwards and wiped away my tears.

"But what am I suppose to do… I can't… do this by myself," I cried.

"I know you think you can't, but God's will, it will never take you where His grace won't keep you. I know you don't understand it all; we rarely do while we're going through it, but sometimes He gotta take you to a place you ain't never been before to get somethin' out of you that you might not know you have. It's in those times... through those life lessons and trials that we learn who we are. Now if you ask me, I think He already done given you some of the answers you need, but you ain't listening 'cause it ain't the answers you wanna hear. Don't shut Him out, baby. You gotta learn to trust Him through it all."

Somewhere in the conversation, I stopped challenging my grandmother and started listening to what she was saying. And she was right, I didn't understand it all, but for the first time in a long time something deep down inside of me wanted to hear all that she was saying.

"Come here, I want you to know that we all make mistakes; that's life. It's not about what you go through, but more so how you handle it. You're a beautiful girl, Gizelle, but that ain't all that you are. You have so much more in you than you give yourself credit for."

"*Ding... dong.*" The chime of the doorbell rang in the background.

"Why don't you go grab that and I'll get the baby settled."

"All right," I said, as I took a deep breath and headed towards the front door. "Who is it?" I asked, as I wiped my eyes and peered through the peep hole. I didn't know if it was my smeared makeup or the cloudiness of the peep hole, but all I could make out was the bottom half of a dark pant leg before it disappeared. I opened the door and couldn't believe my eyes.

"Gizelle... Gizelle!" my grandmother called out. "You lettin' all that air in here on this baby, girl. Who is it?" she hollered.

I wish I could've answered her, but I didn't know myself. All I knew was that shit had just gotten real and if I refused to believe it before, I had no choice but to believe it now. I opened the screen and pulled my black bag inside of the house before opening it. The only thing left on the inside of the bag was a small sheet of folded white paper with the words, *Hope it was good,* scribbled onto it. Damn... what in the hell was going on?!

19

I hated downtown parking, especially on a weekday morning. I arrived at the Federal Courthouse a little after nine, but had to circle the block at least a dozen times before a parking space became available. When one finally opened up, I became just as reckless as some of the other drivers and almost hit a few pedestrians while trying to get over to it. I quickly squeezed behind a Range Rover with a remarkable resemblance to mine, when I realized that lately I had been seeing my fair share of Range Rovers with notable similarities. Not only was this one the same make and model, but we also had identical infant car seats in the back. "Whomever it belongs to has my kind of taste," I thought to myself as I made my way into the courthouse. On the outside I was cool, calm, and collected, but on the inside I was heated, dazed, and confused. Yet and still, I was determined to make sense out of the last twenty-four hours of my life.

"Number four, please," I said to the older gentleman who had just stepped inside of the elevator with me. I walked down the corridor to the courtroom where I had been told Mekhi would appear, and as I went to step inside, the older gentleman who had been in the elevator with me tapped me on my shoulders and said, "Excuse me young lady, but I think you dropped this." I turned around to accept one of the magazines I had been carrying when a folded piece of paper fell from it. The inside of it read, "It's never too late to turn around." I couldn't remember if this was an earlier written note to myself and I didn't have time to contemplate it now, so I continued into the courtroom. Just as I stepped inside, the room began to spin, the lights began to dim, and beads of sweat started to crowd my forehead. Instantly, I felt light-headed and out of breath. I badly wanted to turn back around and walk through the doors I had just come in, but I couldn't move; my feet were planted exactly where I stood.

Was I dreaming? Wake up, Gizelle... please, oh God, wake me up and put me back in the room beside Journey or back at my grandmother's house for another lecture; back at my own house the night before or back in the bed before that awful night of the shooting. Why was I here? Wait! I'm gonna be sick. Oh God, please help me... please, please help me, just this one time and I promise I'll do right from now on…I swear. My mouth became dry right before the saliva sensation started that comes in anticipation of vomit. I felt nervous and fearful at the same time. I turned back around and noticed that there were guards blocking every exit.

"Fuck!" I said to myself, as I heard someone call my name. I slowly turned in the direction the voice was coming from as images from the past twelve months of my life started to flash before my eyes. It all started to make sense as this fuzzy courtroom picture took shape. A half-dozen or more familiar faces, but none that I would've connected until now. My eyes darted around the room as I quickly took attendance. Mehki was up front, to his right were Jeremy and Tracy. Quazi was near the front, Malcolm was in the back, and Yasmine was off to the left holding a newborn dressed in pink. Damn! Why didn't I see this shit coming?

20

Fast Forward...

There I sat, in a courtroom full of so-called acquaintances, feeling devastatingly isolated and deserted, and utterly traumatized with disbelief. I just couldn't believe that shit had panned out in the way that it had. Even more unsettling were the lengths that these rotten motherfuckers had gone to, in order to prove their innocence... and even more so, their betrayal. It all felt like one confusing, elongated nightmare which had stretched way beyond its extremity of vindictiveness. And for what? My hand didn't call for this shit! I wasn't a bad person! I mean sure, I had done some compromising things, but to be deviously and devilishly tricked into the possibility of a chargeable offense seemed to be a position unfit for *any woman* and more particularly, *me*! For hours, I had been quietly sitting and watching, as these fucking vultures, liars, and crooks, collectively intertwined one theatrical performance after the next; all by harnessing tainted images for the sake of their own freedoms. But yet and still, I was the one being accused of *acting* like a goddamn culprit, and consequently waiting for a decision that would impact my entire life. Why didn't I see this shit coming? I saw preludes when it came to every-fuckin'-thing else, but this... this, I would have never expected! I was praying that someone would come shake, nudge, or even jolt me awake from this terrifying nightmare. However, that shit never occurred. Instead the realities of tampering in a *street life,* which brought potential brutal effects, stared me dead in the face as tears slowly started to stream down my cheeks. My disillusioned soul felt heavy with a range of different emotions as I looked up at the woman who ultimately held my fate in her hands and listened intently as she began to speak.

"Well, Ms. Sadiq, do you understand the role you played in all of this?" the judge asked before quickly continuing. "Here's the thing and here's what I've come to learn about your generation, in particular the females born from it. You all allow yourselves to be put into this repetitive cycle of self-destruction which continuously perpetuates a lifestyle filled with fast money and fast cars. But, what you fail to realize is that anything that comes too easy, is too easy! Now sure, the guys do their part but, for no other reason I'm sure is pure laziness, competition, ego, and male pride. But, what *you, young lady, need* to realize is that when you take what someone is giving, just because he's giving it, he takes a part of your essence, simply because *you* allow him to. What I wish, no implore that you all would do, is start demanding more for and out of yourselves and stop letting people or situations define your existence. I can only hope that you take this time to find yourself so that you will have a clear understanding of life's morals and principles before passing this same attitude down to your son. I hereby sentence you to sixty months in a women's correctional facility. Court is dismissed."

I cringed as she spat out her last statements and struggled hard not to cry. What had I done that was so wrong and how in the hell did I ever get to this point? I looked down at the note pad in which I had scribbled a few words and silently read over the lines as my tears began to fall…

Haven't seen what I have seen,
or lived how I have lived
yet, some are always first to scream,
exactly what they would have did!
Did the best that I could do,

with the best I could've done...
Tried not involving you,
just sacrificed my fun
and choices that were made...
were for me and my little one!
Troubles don't last always,
that, they preach when Sundays come,
try holding on to faith, stand straight, and walk,
don't ever run!
For this too, you'll overcome...
when it's all said and finally done,
greater He who is in you, who has forsaken' His
only son,
greater He who is in you, who has forsaken' His
only son...

...to be continued...